WRAITH OF V

Contemplating a scheme to plunder a sinister Venetian island of a rumoured hoard, a tour company advisor finds more there than he bargained for . . . The group gathered for the reading of a will get the shock of their lives . . . A distant oil-drilling platform endures a bizarre siege . . . A man undergoes a hideous transformation . . . The night shift in a morgue takes a deadly turn . . . In an English village on All Hallows Eve, an ancient evil reawakens. Six tales of horror and the macabre by Edmund Glasby.

EDMUND GLASBY

WRAITH OF VENGEANCE
& Other Stories

Complete and Unabridged

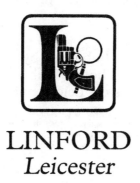

LINFORD
Leicester

First published in Great Britain

First Linford Edition
published 2019

*A catalogue record for this book is available
from the British Library.*

ISBN 978–1–4448–3984–5

Published by
F. A. Thorpe (Publishing)
Anstey, Leicestershire

Set by Words & Graphics Ltd.
Anstey, Leicestershire
Printed and bound in Great Britain by
T. J. International Ltd., Padstow, Cornwall

This book is printed on acid-free paper

WRAITH OF VENGEANCE

The water taxi finally glided to a halt beside a landing point and Michael Harper, thirty-one, fair-haired and smartly dressed, breathed a sigh of relief. The journey from Marco Polo airport to Venice had been longer and choppier than he had anticipated. With the November mist obscuring most of the lagoon, he could only see the channel markers and the murky waters, none of the beauty of the city they called *La Serenissima* — 'the most serene' — that he had hoped for. At least the journey was over and he was in plenty of time for a light supper somewhere before the early night he needed.

Accepting his suitcase from the pilot, he asked for a recommendation for good Venetian food, not too expensive. The pilot smiled broadly at his fluent but heavily accented Italian. 'You should try Raffaele's, straight down this canal. Proper food, and they won't rip you off like some!'

Half an hour later, savouring a particularly good meal, Harper felt fully recovered and ready to start work. He was never sure how to describe his career and generally just said he worked in tourism. It was his job to scout out places where his company could set up package holidays with a cultural theme. British tourists of a certain age were more interested than ever before in exploring Europe as long as it was made easy for them, and his youthful adventures travelling abroad had suited him well to the task of researcher.

Harper had one week to work out the best value tours — appraising the hotels, restaurants, places of cultural and historical interest, local entertainment — and to make the contacts that, from his past experiences in Paris, Barcelona and Rome, would prove invaluable.

In the off-season, he looked for new destinations. In the summer, he took his turn as tour guide and manager, which allowed him to revisit his favourite cities.

Finishing his coffee, he chatted a little with the waiter about the tourist trade.

Then, after having paid his bill, he left Raffaele's, buttoning his coat against the chilly, damp night air. For some inexplicable reason, he experienced a growing sense of unease as he walked down the narrow alleys. On either side of him, dilapidated buildings and decaying shop fronts loomed up like towering shadows. In the thickening gloom, ghostly figures passed by, going about their unknown business, their presence heard rather than seen in the deepening fog.

Whether due to his day's travelling or his surroundings, a feeling of nausea began to fester in his stomach, and with every step the visibility decreased. The tang of seawater added to his sickness. From far off, he could hear the sepulchral tolling of a church bell; its baleful, echoing tones full of melancholy.

Turning a corner, he caught the tenebrous image of someone in a rather grotesque carnival mask and hooded cloak. A moment later it was gone.

★   ★   ★

The tourist office off the Piazza San Marco was quiet at this time of year — in fact when he turned up the following morning, Harper gathered he was lucky to find anyone in — but his decent grasp of Italian and his natural charm stood him in good stead with the female official as he asked for the lowdown on the various tour guides and attractions. Finally, he asked who would be a good person to take him around the lagoon so he could check out the other islands.

'You'll want to talk to Arturo Pozzi. He's been piloting the lagoon for thirty years and knows everything, or says he does. Just make sure that you set a price for the trip in advance, for he's a bit of a rogue.'

'He sounds like just the person I need. Where can I find him?'

'At this time of day he'll be up and out working, but he always goes to a little trattoria just round the corner for lunch. You should find him there at about one o'clock. Tell him I recommended him.' The woman laughed. 'That should encourage him to quote you a decent price.' She turned to the pile of brochures she had been putting together for Harper. 'These will give you the basic information about Venice, but by all means come back when you have any more questions.'

'Thank you, signora, I will. You've been most helpful.' Harper smiled, left the small, rather fusty office, and breathed the fresh air of the piazza gratefully. He decided to locate the trattoria first, and was heading in the right direction when he heard a cry from one of the narrow alleyways. Peering down it, he could see a couple of polizia crouched on the pavement, pulling something unsavoury out of the canal. Curious, Harper walked quietly in their direction. He came to an abrupt halt when he realised that the sodden object they were hauling up was a pale and bloated corpse. The two uniformed men swore at the sight but did not seem that surprised. He pressed himself into the wall of the alleyway and strained his ears to listen.

'It's Stefano Gritti, isn't it?'

'Definitely. God, I hate this! It looks just like the others — you can see the burns.'

'I'll go back to the station in order to get the team out. The sooner we can get this cordoned off, the better.'

From his vantage point, Harper decided it would be sensible to leave. The last thing he wanted was to get caught up in a crime scene, however interesting. The trattoria was still closed but he found a cafe nearby, ordered a coffee and tried to turn his mind back to his work. After ten minutes reading up on the Gallerie dell'Academia, he gave up and looked around for a likely gossip. A few tables away a middle-aged man, probably retired, was leafing through a newspaper. Harper rose and politely asked where he could buy a paper.

'You can have this one soon; it belongs to the cafe.' The man drained his cup and turned to the sports pages.

'It's just that I saw something rather unsettling this morning,' Harper said, certain that this would pique the Venetian's interest.

'Oh yes?'

Briefly, Harper explained about the body in the canal.

'Dear God, another one!' the man

exclaimed. 'Bruno!' he called out to the waiter. 'It would appear they've found another body!'

The waiter came hurrying over, and soon the story came out. There had been three unsolved murders that autumn, all with the same *modus operandi*. The victims had been found in the water, burn marks on their bodies. All had drowned.

'Does anybody know if there's any connection between them?' Harper asked, fascinated by this modern-day mystery.

'In life, you mean? Not really. Two men, one woman. All normal people, it seems. They tried to suggest suicide at first.'

'That's right,' the waiter agreed. 'They were all Venetians of course, not tourists, but apart from that, nothing. Oh, a customer! I must leave you.' He shook hands and went back to his work.

Harper checked his watch and saw that it was nearly lunchtime. He pushed his chair back. 'Thank you for the conversation. All this hardly seems possible in such a beautiful city, but I suppose people are people everywhere and the worst in human nature is always with us.'

'True, my friend, although the authorities are trying to play it down in the press. Bad for business.'

Harper laughed a little wryly.

★　★　★

The trattoria had a few customers, all of whom appeared to be locals, so Harper asked the waiter if Arturo Pozzi was there.

'Yes, he's just come in. Over there by the window.'

Harper walked over and introduced himself to the stocky, dark-haired, broad-shouldered Italian and they were soon haggling over a price for a quick tour of the lagoon.

Pozzi's grin grew more pronounced as he realised that Harper was no pushover. Finally, he laughed. '*Va bene!* I'll do it for your price if you buy me a few beers afterwards.'

Harper smiled and shook the other's offered hand, wincing somewhat at the tight grip. It was then that he noticed the gleaming gold rings on the man's fingers.

10

They were of a quality he would not have expected to see on a man of his profession. He could not help but think that this man, underneath his friendly veneer, probably had connections with some of the more nefarious outfits in Venice. 'That sounds all right to me. When can we start?'

'It's lunchtime. You can't hurry an Italian over his food! Have something yourself and then we'll set off.'

Harper ordered a risotto and they chatted about Venice. Considering his new contact, he decided that Pozzi undoubtedly *was*, as he had been informed, a rogue; a larger-than-life character. Harper was reminded of several other men he knew in various cities who had been most helpful with both his work and his hobby. By two o'clock they were ready to go and walked off to Pozzi's motorboat.

'We have to go slowly round the main islands, but I can show you a bit of speed when we get further out,' Pozzi said as he jumped into the boat. 'We'll do Murano and Burano first, then come back down to the Lido if there's time before it gets dark. Then tomorrow, I will take you round Venice herself. I guarantee you won't find a better guide.'

Harper climbed into the boat more cautiously, reflecting that water travel really was not for him. He needed to decide which sights would go on his draft itinerary, however, and he could see he would get a good condensed history from Pozzi.

True to his boast, Pozzi talked knowledgably and amusingly, both in Italian and English. Harper wrote quickly in his notebook while watching the scenery. There was no fog today, and the place was far closer to his mental image than before. In summer it would be stunning, if rather too hot. Maybe spring would be a good time to bring the first group of tourists over. He was mulling things over when he realised Pozzi had changed the subject.

' . . . always been a dark side to Venice, right up to the present. These last few months, three poor souls have been dragged out of the water, murdered for sure — whatever they tried to say about suicide.'

Having listened attentively for an hour with only a few interjected questions, Harper could not help but take some delight in being better informed, on one subject at least, than his guide. He put his notebook down and said: 'It's four now, I'm afraid.'

'*What?* Tell me,' Pozzi demanded eagerly, slowing the boat's engine in order to listen. As he explained, Harper could see a change in Pozzi's manner.

'Are you sure they said Stefano Gritti?' his guide asked intently.

'Yes. I'm sorry, did you know him?'

'I hadn't actually met him, but . . . ' Pozzi looked uncertain. 'I knew of him. In fact I was due to meet him tomorrow evening. He has a shop in Venice; artefacts, antiques, you know? I sometimes do a little business with the traders.'

Harper looked at him shrewdly. His instinct about Pozzi seemed to be correct. Casually, he asked a little more about the nature of the extra bit of 'business' the Venetian did, and Pozzi admitted that he dealt in antiques of a dubious nature. Sometimes fakes, though more often they were genuine but of 'imperfect' provenance.

'A few of us keep our eyes and ears open for interesting items. A little money changes hands. It's no big deal.' Pozzi sounded defensive.

Harper smiled broadly. 'Then you may have heard of Vincenzo Faradi in Rome? He's a good friend of mine. We've done a lot of business over the years.'

Pozzi stared for a moment, then burst out laughing. He slapped Harper on the arm. 'So, you're one of us, my friend.'

'In my spare time. When I was younger, travelling Europe and running out of money, I stumbled across a seventeenth-century silver cup in France, and the money came in very handy. Since then, I'll admit to helping my luck along from time to time with this and that.'

'Well perhaps you will be 'lucky' in Venice, and if you need to sell something, just let me know.'

Harper nodded. Faradi was a fence with a reputation amongst thieves for complete discretion, and his name opened certain doors. Harper had found his travelling lifestyle offered him opportunities to smuggle small valuable items around Europe, and his eye for quality had stood him in good stead.

'But enough of that for now,' he said. 'Do you think there's any connection between Gritti's lifestyle, shall we say, and his death? If there's any chance that someone's targeting people like us, then my persona in Venice will have to be whiter than white.'

Now that the boat was moving slowly, Pozzi opened a small cupboard and drew out a bottle of grappa and two glass tumblers. Pouring them both a drink, his face grew grim again. 'I wouldn't think so. The other two men were both respectable citizens; a market stall-holder near the Rialto, and a warehouse man. I think the woman was a retired nurse.' He raised his glass. 'To Gritti.'

Harper echoed the toast and tried not to wince at the strong undoubtedly homemade alcohol. Pozzi swallowed his in one gulp.

'Shall we leave the tourist side of your visit for a bit?' The Italian asked after stowing the bottle and glasses away. 'There's a man I know out on the Lido who I think you would like to meet. I also think I should tell him about Gritti. It may have repercussions for him.'

* * *

A little while later, Harper and Pozzi entered a small nondescript house stuffed to the rafters with a mixture of antiques and junk. They were greeted by a slim bespectacled elderly man, furnished with coffee and biscuits, and firmly seated on a beautiful if slightly battered chaise longue. Signor Adesto clearly liked to get some use out of his stock. As they drank, Pozzi told the tale of Gritti's death — with a few embellishments of his own, Harper noticed with good humour.

Adesto sipped his coffee, listening attentively, his face grave. Finally he set the cup down with a sigh. 'Thank you for telling me this. I shall have to contact a few others who were doing business with him. There will be loose ends to tie up.' He rubbed his hand wearily over his face. 'I hope that I am mistaken, but I believe that he may have been partly to blame for his terrible misfortune.'

'What! What do you know?' Pozzi demanded eagerly.

Adesto shifted pensively in his chair and looked almost embarrassed, but after a pause he continued: 'You know Gritti's shop; a small place with his favourite legitimate pieces on display? Well, he ran out of room there a few years ago and asked if I could recommend anywhere to store his extra items, in particular the more dubious things that he has been moving around in the last decade or so.' He smiled briefly and gestured at the room. 'I replied, 'Why ask me? Do I look like I keep my stock in storage?' Gritti laughed at that but continued to press me on the matter. He desperately needed somewhere secure. There had been too many questions from the authorities, and he was feeling the heat. I suggested a few people he could ask and he thanked me and was about to leave when he suddenly stopped and seemed transfixed by the view from my window. A moment later he laughed and exclaimed, 'Perfect!''

Harper and Pozzi both glanced out the window in question, but the light was fading and Harper could make out little. Pozzi, however, turned quickly back. 'Not Poveglia!' he exclaimed in disbelief.

'That's what I said to Gritti, but he was excited. Said it was the perfect place.'

'Excuse me, but what *is* Poveglia?' Harper interjected with interest.

Reaching for a small gold crucifix that hung on a chain around his neck, Pozzi gave it a quick kiss, then jabbed his finger towards the window. 'That island you can just see in the dusk. It is abandoned now, off limits to those without authority.'

'Well, I can see how that might appeal for a secret store.'

'It is the reason why it is abandoned that is the problem. The whole island is a damned grave!' Pozzi explained.

Signor Adesto took up the tale. 'Poveglia has had a bad connection with the plague over the centuries. They say it was the Romans who first used some of the smaller islands to dump infected bodies, and it was certainly one of the islands used as a place to quarantine visitors during the time of the Black Death in the Middle Ages. Then it became used as a site to burn the bodies of the victims of plague. Not a bad idea in itself; but when the plague was at its worst, when people were hysterical with fear, it is said that they did not always wait for the victims to die. The plague doctors and the pizzicamorti — the corpse-bearers and the specialist gravediggers — had the authority to take away both the dead and the living who were suspected of infection. Some unfortunates were actually burnt or buried alive.'

'Dear God!' Harper exclaimed in disgust.

'It was a very dark time for Venice. I daresay there are hundreds, if not thousands, of remains to be found if one digs deep on several of our islands, and several pits where they buried bodies in lime, even here on the Lido. But that is not all as far as Poveglia is concerned. The tale gets darker still; for you see, it has not been properly inhabited for centuries. No one wants to live there. Napoleon continued its use for quarantine, and it once had a lighthouse; given the lack of space in Venice, you would expect someone to settle there. It has a bad atmosphere. Death has always clung to the island. Bones are occasionally picked up in the nets of those fishermen who dare venture close to it, and the ground itself is thick with ash — the cremated remains of thousands. And, would you believe, in the twenties they set up a sanatorium for the mentally sick. It was not long before the patients — and the staff working there — started claiming they saw the spirits of the plague victims.'

The old man shook his head sadly, then carried on. 'The last, and probably worst, episode in the island's history happened not that long ago. A doctor there went mad, torturing the patients, experimenting on them, carrying out unsanctioned lobotomies and things like that. He was a sadist. He made out that he was trying to cure them through pioneering new methods, but no one believed him. Then *he* started seeing the ghosts. In the end, he threw himself off the bell-tower. A rumour began that he survived the fall but was strangled by a malign mist as punishment for his deeds.' Adesto sighed wearily. 'Several years ago they closed the island completely, and I thanked God for the decision. It is a wicked place with an evil history. As I said, no one sane will go there.'

Harper sat in stunned silence for a moment, listening to this modern-day ghost story. He felt uncomfortable at the macabre tale and the proximity of the island. He had never dreamed there was such a dark side to Venice.

Pozzi pushed himself to his feet and declared they needed another coffee. As he clattered about, clearly at home in the house, Harper wondered if Gritti had truly used that godforsaken place to hide stolen goods. Many of the Italians he knew were deeply religious and superstitious, and to them it would be unthinkable. Then again, greed was a great motivator. He knew that only too well. Surely, though, there could be no connection between Gritti's death and that accursed island.

When Pozzi brought in the coffees and the inevitable bottle of grappa, he voiced his thoughts.

'That, my friend,' began Pozzi, 'brings us to the manner of Gritti's death — and the other three, for that matter. You said he had been burnt and that the others had marks as well. That fact was in the newspapers. When the patients in the mental hospital reported seeing ghosts, they babbled of half-burnt corpses. You see, when some of the gravely ill were prematurely flung onto the fire, they had just enough life to try to escape and would make for the water. Once there, they invariably drowned, which brings us back to the recent deaths — drowned but with extensive burns.'

'I admit that's a little suggestive,' Harper conceded with a certain level of scepticism in his tone.

'There is also another connection between Poveglia and the deaths. Signora Donata, the second victim, was a retired nurse. What they didn't say was that she worked for a while at the asylum. Gritti knew her from when she helped out with his elderly mother.'

Harper nodded slowly. 'I see your point. If Gritti was visiting Poveglia with her help, and maybe the other victims as well, might someone have seen it as insulting to the dead?'

'It *is* insulting!' Pozzi exclaimed. 'But you would have to be mad to kill for it.'

'Anyone who murders four people may well be mad.' Adesto looked keenly at both of them. 'The question now is, do we tell the authorities?'

★ ★ ★

They stayed a long time with Adesto, debating whether he had a duty to tell the police of Gritti's activities on Poveglia. On one side of the argument, there was no hard evidence to link the island with his death or those of the others, and it would necessitate some very awkward questions about Adesto's own line of work. On the other, if there was a madman about and this information could catch him, then they should say something. The discussion circled for the rest of the evening — through a simple supper concocted by Pozzi and a large number of cigarettes. Eventually Adesto had decided that duty might be served by an anonymous tip-off through a friend who owed him a favour.

Pozzi and Harper went back across the bitterly cold moonlit lagoon. The mist had returned, making the air hazy with shafts of moonlight illuminating the drifting vapour.

'So that's Poveglia,' Harper said quietly as they neared the unpopulated island. It was in complete darkness, a stark contrast to the other islands of the lagoon; and there seemed to be a smell in the air, faint yet slightly foul. He shivered. For the first time since arriving in Venice, he began to feel as though he was getting a little out of his depth.

Pozzi slowed the boat so they could take a better look. Moonlight fell eerily on the tall bell-tower, and it was possible to make out a few buildings but little else and they contemplated the view in silence for a time.

Pozzi finally spoke, voicing the thoughts

that hung in the air between them. 'Tomorrow this place will be crawling with police searching for Gritti's hoard.'

'And for clues about the murders,' Harper put in.

'I wonder where he stashed things? There can't be that many buildings that would be suitable.' Pozzi was eyeing the island speculatively.

For a moment, Harper was sorely tempted by the suggestion that Pozzi was obviously hinting at — to go ashore to search for the hoard themselves. A few hours' work to find it and get the most portable items in the boat, and they could make a lot of money. Staring at Poveglia, he had almost opened his mouth to say 'Let's go for it' when he felt a shudder of revulsion at the memory of Gritti's bloated body being hauled out of the water. Although he was an opportunistic thief, Harper's main drive was self-preservation, and no prize was worth risking his life. His decision made, he cleared his throat and spoke. 'You know, it's quite possible that the murderer is living there, sleeping on one of the old hospital beds or even lying atop Gritti's stolen goods. Additionally, how do we know that this is the act of one person? Could be that there's an organised gang behind all of this.'

'It's possible.' Pozzi nodded his head. 'Let's get out of here. Poveglia can keep its treasure.'

They finished the evening in a bar, trying to lift the mood. Arranging to meet the next day, Pozzi had clasped Harper's hand, saying, 'Tomorrow I will show you the beauty of Venice. You have seen too much of her ugly side today.'

★ ★ ★

Harper woke the following morning feeling distinctly jaded. At breakfast, he picked up the morning paper and was unsurprised to see that the death of Gritti had made the front page. Gritti was currently being described as a local businessman, which he supposed was the truth, if not the whole truth. There was no attempt made by the police to suggest suicide this time. Presumably Adesto would get his message through today, and Poveglia would receive an official visit. He thought briefly, wistfully, of the stash that might be hidden somewhere on the island. He knew the thought had crossed Pozzi's mind as well, but there was no chance of a trip out there with the police around — even if their consciences had allowed it. No, today he would be the respectable Michael Harper, tourism expert; and if Pozzi happened to introduce him to any interesting dealers, well that was just getting to know the locals. As he rose from the table, he suddenly remembered a strange dream from the night before — a masked, cloaked figure in the mist and a faint sound of jingling bells. A shiver ran through him at the memory, though why it should, he could not tell. Dismissing the odd fearful feeling, he set out for his meeting with Pozzi.

★　★　★

They could not have asked for a better day for the time of year. It was bright and crisp, lifting both men's spirits as they walked through the wonderful city. It turned out that Pozzi did indeed know his business, and he brought life to each street, church and canal with a storyteller's flair. By unspoken agreement, they did not mention Gritti or Poveglia all morning. Stopping for lunch at a place owned by Pozzi's cousin, they worked out an itinerary for the afternoon that made Harper's feet ache at the prospect. He would have to factor in some trips on the vaporetto for his tourists, that was for sure.

By three o'clock, they had made their way to the Arsenale in the east — the old naval area; and Harper was greatly relieved when Pozzi hailed a water taxi to take them back to the centre. As Pozzi chatted with the pilot, Harper leafed through a rather lurid history book which had been left on the seat.

As the pages flicked idly past his eyes, he suddenly stopped and opened the book flat. It was the rather ghastly-looking figure he had seen in his dream, cloaked and with its face obscured by a black hat, a hood with cut-out eyeholes and an unflattering bird-beaked mask. Harper felt the sense of unease again and started to read the accompanying text.

The pizzicamorti: corpse-bearers who dealt with victims of the plague. The elongated nose of the mask was packed with herbs thought to prevent them from becoming infected. The all-encompassing floor-length oil-skinned cloak and gloves provided a barrier when moving corpses. The pizzicamorti also wore small bells on their ankles, the sound alerting the public to their presence.

Harper stared at the worryingly familiar image. He had not realised the gruesome tales of Poveglia had affected him so much, for surely this had precipitated his dream. He must have seen this image or one like it somewhere on his travels and noted it unconsciously, for he certainly did not recall having seen it before. Strangely, in the picture the cloak swept all the way to the ground — so how had he known about the bells?

'Ah, you see?' The pilot pointed triumphantly to Harper, seemingly fascinated by his book. 'People are drawn by the horrible just as much as the wonderful. I tell you, a ghost tour in Venice at night would make good money.'

Pozzi looked with some concern at Harper. 'Are you all right? You're a bad colour.'

'Seasick on a canal. That would be embarrassing.' Harper tried to make light of it, but he felt hot and nauseous. He had just remembered that he had also seen a figure like that on his first night in Venice, before he had even known of its plague-ridden past. A coincidence certainly, but . . .

'We've done a lot today; and after last night, well . . . it must be catching up with you.' Pozzi gave the other a bottle of water. 'Here, take this, and then I think you should get some rest.'

*　★　★

Harper fell into bed, deciding to do without food and rather hoping to sleep it off, whatever *it* was. After a couple of hours of welcome oblivion, the dream returned.

He was staggering along a badly lit alley somewhere in Venice, and from behind him came the sound of bells; not church bells, but rather little eerily jingling ones. There was a pain in his side, and looking down he saw blood seeping through his shirt. He knew that to stop running would be fatal, but his strength was failing and his vision blurring. The rough walls of the alley seemed to batter him from one side to the other as he lurched like a drunkard. It was night, or very early morning, and the place was deserted.

Stumbling, Harper turned a corner and found himself in an enclosed courtyard. Frantically, he scanned the area for a way out — a door, a tree near a wall, anything. There was no way out! The sound of the bells continued to come ever closer, and his heartbeat was accelerating rapidly.

His fear intensified as he could now make out the sound of footsteps and the faint scraping sound of a heavy cloak dragging its edge along the ground. Shaking terribly, Harper made ready to try to push past the horror and run, if he could, back to somewhere safe. As he turned to make a dash for it, his pursuer swept round the corner into the court-yard. Harper staggered back and lost his footing, landing heavily on the ground. Staring in terror at the pizzicamorti, he could see nothing of the other's face at all. It was completely covered by the outlandish proboscis-like mask and a broad-brimmed hat.

As the figure drew closer, Harper shrieked, 'I'm not dead, you can't take me!'

But the pizzicamorti reached out for him with its gloved hands. He tried to move, but his legs refused to work. He tried to fight it off with his hands but it implacably grabbed his arms, sending a wave of revulsion and horror through him.

Twisting ineffectually, sobbing with terror, he shouted with all his might in the thing's face: 'DON'T TAKE ME! I'M NOT DEAD!'

★ ★ ★

Harper sprang awake. His heart was pounding, and sweat and tears ran down his face. Trembling, he fumbled with the bedside light, almost knocking it over before he got it switched on. Hugging his knees to his chest, he fought to calm himself, to stop the almost heart-stopping fear that threatened to overwhelm him. He had never experienced anything like this before, not even in childhood. Trying to breathe deeply, to let the adrenaline dissipate, he gradually succeeded in regaining control of his mind and body.

When he was able, he took a shower and dressed, knowing there was no chance of getting back to sleep that night. As he sat on the bed, smoking the rest of his cigarettes, he decided that the nightmare must be due to overwork or stress. He had heard many gruesome stories in his time, both from ancient history and more recent events. Nothing had ever had this effect on him before. Vowing to take some time off, perhaps visit his parents in England after this trip, he waited for the sun to rise behind his closed curtains. Rational though he was trying to be, nothing would make him look out into the darkened courtyard below until the sun was up. For deep down he was convinced that if he did, he would find himself staring into the frightening, long-snouted face of the pizzicamorti.

★ ★ ★

'Have you heard? They've caught the murderer!' The owner of the hotel greeted Harper excitedly as he took his usual table for breakfast. 'Some madman was tracked to the island of Poveglia, over by the Lido last night. They caught him trying to kill himself!'

Harper felt a huge surge of relief wash over him. Hopefully this news would sort out his subconscious. 'Tell me more,' he said, gesturing the landlady to join him.

Dumping the breakfast tray unceremoniously down on the table, she drew an extra chair over, happy to share the gossip. Very few hotels stayed open in

Venice in the winter, and he had already deduced that the owner here did so mostly because she liked the company.

'The paper has some facts, but the rumours fly faster than arrows in this place. The postman said he heard that the police had a tip-off that a couple of the victims were criminals using the island to hide drugs or guns.' She talked matter-of-factly while pouring them both a coffee.

Harper stifled a smile. The 'Chinese whispers' nature of rumours and gossip was doing its usual job of gradually twisting the truth. No doubt the killings and everything else would be levelled at the Mafia in the end.

'I didn't think Venice had much trouble with that kind of thing,' Harper commented, starting on a bread roll.

'Up until now, maybe. This could be the tip of the iceberg.'

'You say that they got the man before he could kill himself?' Harper prompted her to continue.

'Yes. Apparently they saw him leap onto a burning bonfire, but managed to drag him off and into the water before he died. He's under armed guard at the hospital now. He must have been really crazy. The paper suggested he might have been a patient at the awful asylum that used to be there. If so, I almost feel sorry for him.'

'I think I'm just glad he's been stopped!' Harper exclaimed.

'I know, but evil begets evil. I could tell you tales about that place. Tales that would make your skin crawl.'

Harper hastily declined the offer. He had no wish to add to his nightmares.

★   ★   ★

Wandering through Venice that morning, the news was everywhere, the facts slowly emerging from the speculation as the day progressed. By lunchtime it was being reported that the murderer, one Guido Maletta, was the brother of the nurse, Signora Donata, and had been seen taking his boat in the direction of the island. The matter appeared to be clinched by a witness who claimed that the first victim, the market-stall holder, had used Maletta as a porter on several occasions. The working theory seemed to be that all of the dead had been up to no good and had perhaps tried to double-cross Maletta.

Every shop and cafe buzzed with the revelations; and while Harper was relieved that the man had been caught, he wished they would stop talking about it. By four o'clock, he heard on a radio that Maletta had died from his burns, but the news did not halt the endless speculation. As the day gave way to night, he felt sick to death of the whole story. A quiet meal somewhere and a bottle of wine to ensure a good night's sleep were what he needed. Remembering a restaurant he had seen earlier, he set off in search of peace and relaxation.

★   ★   ★

Two hours and a lot of wine later, he was well on the way to a heavy night's sleep, if not a good one, and he seemed to be developing a taste for grappa. The alcohol was providing him with an illusion of warmth, and although he was a little unsteady on his feet, it was not far to the hotel. Carrying his heavy coat over one arm, he crossed a small bridge and turned into a narrow alley. The streetlights were spaced further apart here, with pools of darker shadow in-between. In one of these dim patches, Harper stumbled slightly, and to his annoyance turned his ankle. Caught off balance, he pitched awkwardly against the wall, swearing as he felt something scrape painfully along his side. He had ripped his clothes against a bit of broken masonry, and the stone had rasped a short but fairly deep cut just below his ribs. As he gingerly investigated the wound, he heard a sound that made him catch his breath and freeze — a faint tinkle of bells behind him.

Spinning round, he scanned the misty alley, searching the shadows. There was no one visible, but he still heard the bells — a rhythmic jingle that marked out a steady walking pace. It had to be a dream again, Harper thought frantically. It was just as before. The only thing missing was the stalking figure. Suddenly, he was aware of a cold insistent voice in his head telling him he was not asleep; urging him to run.

He broke into an unsteady jog, his heart pounding, his ribs aching. His ankle stabbed with pain as he put his weight on it, but he forced himself to override it. The bells seemed to be getting louder, and he could not stop himself from glancing back every few strides. At first, there was nothing to be seen; but the third time he looked, he saw a spectral shadow in the mist about twenty feet behind him, its outline horrifyingly familiar.

Panting with the effort and the terror that were flooding his body with adrenaline, Harper staggered on, rounded a corner and let out a sob. He was in the courtyard from his dream. There was no way out. Panicked thoughts whirled through his brain. This was impossible. Either that, or he was imagining it . . . or else he must be asleep.

As his mind battled to present alternative explanations, his eyes were dragged to the archway of the courtyard, and he saw the impossible — the faint human shape that drifted in began to solidify, and he saw the long heavy cloak, the broad-brimmed hat and the grotesque bird-beaked mask. Harper collapsed to the ground, his strength failing as horror overtook him.

The pizzicamorti reached out for him . . .

★ ★ ★

It was the sound of screaming that brought Harper out of his dark oblivion. He struggled to wake, like a diver making for the surface. Forcing his eyes to open, he saw a blaze of light a short way off. Pushing himself up onto his knees, he found the source of the screams — the pizzicamorti was dragging a man towards the huge bonfire that burned near to a building he recognised with a sickening lurch of his stomach. It was unmistakably the bell-tower on Poveglia.

As he realised this, Harper also recognised the screamer. It was Pozzi — trying with all his might to resist his would-be murderer, battering him with his fists and struggling like a fish caught on a hook, convulsing his body to get free. His frenzied efforts were having no effect at all, and he was being edged closer and closer to the flames.

Harper staggered to his feet, unsure for a moment whether to try to help or to use the opportunity to escape. As he wavered, Pozzi caught sight of him and began shouting hysterically, 'Stop him! Help me! For God's sake, help me!'

The pizzicamorti turned his head to look at Harper, and Pozzi's flailing hands caught its mask and tore it off. In the light from the bonfire, they saw a swirling mist pour out, and then glimpsed the face behind — *but it was not one face, it was many.* Just as Harper made out one visage, it morphed into another. There were the faces of men, women and children: white, black, young and old and all were deformed and diseased, and all were in agony.

Pozzi cried out in horror and finally managed to wrench himself from the many-faced fiend's grip, falling heavily to the ground. Harper felt the bile rise in his throat and was struggling not to throw up. The mist was continuing to spread out, flowing over Pozzi as he scrambled to escape the clutching hands. It surrounded him completely, wrapping around his body like a shroud, muffling his sobs of terror.

The shock and fear had almost paralysed him, but now Harper did his best to run towards the bonfire, hoping to push the pizzicamorti into it. Whether it would do any good he had no idea, but it might buy him time to assist Pozzi and get off this damned island.

Pozzi was completely engulfed by the strange mist now and was being hefted onto the shoulder of the demonic corpse-bearer, struggling weakly.

Harper slowed his pace, frantically trying to work out what to do. If he cannoned into them, it could make Pozzi fall into the fire. If he did nothing, the thing would surely throw him on anyway. Shaking with exhaustion and fear, he changed his direction to try to get between Pozzi and the bonfire. Hoping to distract the pizzicamorti, he started to shout at it. 'Why are you doing this?' he yelled. 'What are you?' To his surprise, the thing paused and turned to face him.

Its continuously melting features seemed to consider the questions before answering in a voice that was a doom-laden choir of pain-wracked sobs. An unholy orchestra of tortured souls screeched out of the thing's mouth. 'We are the murdered, the tormented, the abandoned. All those who were killed here by the uncaring, the fearful and the cruel.'

'But why are you attacking us? We're not your murderers!' Harper panted, resisting the urge to cover his ears and block out the voice that seemed to be tearing its way through his brain.

'This is our grave you have defiled. It is where both the living and the dead were interred.' The pizzicamorti wailed, swaying slightly as if it too was tired. 'It should be sacred, but they keep coming here — wanting to use this island for their own gain. They brought yet more doomed souls and a tormentor. The pain . . . ' It broke off and let the now unmoving body of Pozzi fall to the ground as if distracted. 'The pain of those wretches . . . betrayed by a doctor . . . was too much. It called on us to take revenge and ensure the sanctity of this place forever.'

Harper realised it must mean the asylum with its demented doctor. From what he recalled of the legend, he too had been strangled by a strange mist. How this knowledge could help him escape from the vengeful conglomeration of spirits that had assumed a solitary form, he did not know. But surely he himself had done no wrong? How could he be to blame? 'Great wrongs were done here, I've heard, but my friend and I aren't part of it. Please, let us go, and the island will be peaceful again.'

The pizzicamorti began to move, swinging its head around as if in pain. 'None may come here. You have violated this place with your presence. The thieves thought to use our graves for their own gain, and you also want to take what you can. We know this.' It gestured to itself, moving jerkily. 'This vessel carries us with it, giving us the power we never had at our deaths.' Its voice rose in a grating crescendo of cries. 'None will desecrate our graves anymore!'

Harper began to back away, sweat breaking out on his skin as he tried to frame a denial. 'I'd never set foot here until you brought me. I have no interest in Poveglia.'

'*WE KNOW YOU!*' the entity shrieked. 'You would have plundered. You would have scattered our bones and turned over our ashes. We saw the greed in your heart!' It bent down, hauled Pozzi up and, before Harper could do anything, flung him into the thick of the bonfire.

'*No!*' Harper cried out in horror, starting instinctively towards the fire, desperately hoping he could drag Pozzi off. The burning man let out an appalling, tormented scream. With a strength born of desperation, Pozzi, blazing and smoking, threw himself off the fire and went stumbling towards the water. Harper rushed to follow him, hoping he could somehow save them both; but he had already realised that this was how all the others had died. Even Maletta had undoubtedly been thrown onto the fire by the crazed phantom who Harper knew could not always be seen, and the police had naturally assumed he had tried to kill himself.

Pozzi had collapsed a few feet from the water's edge and was not moving when Harper reached him. He dragged the smoking man the rest of the way, his eyes alert for movement from the pizzicamorti. The thing had not moved or spoken since Pozzi had leapt from the bonfire, and it seemed to be waiting for something. Supporting Pozzi in the freezing water, Harper tried to check for a pulse, but his own frantically beating heart was thundering in his ears. 'Come on, wake up!' he begged, trying not to look too much at the blistered flesh on one side of the other's face.

'He is gone.' The hideous whisper suddenly sounded horrifically close behind him. 'And you will follow.'

Before Harper could scream, let alone run, the mist closed in around him, solidifying like cement. Then he did scream, as he was hauled inexorably to the bonfire. Struggling, sobbing and begging with helpless terror, he could do nothing as the spectre of Poveglia pushed him into the centre of the fire.

The pizzicamorti watched his agonies dispassionately. Finally, the embodiment of the deaths of thousands rolled Harper's blackened, twitching body into the dark water of the lagoon and waited. As the last vestiges of life left Harper, the thing stooped and picked up its beaked mask.

Others would come . . . and others would pay the same price.

WHERE THERE'S
A WILL . . .

*Three days after Babette LaVey died,
something terrible was born.*

A chill night darkness hugged the trailing branches of the black mangroves, and a writhing mist rose clammily from the sluggish swamp. The moon was little more than a white patch stained against the boiling clouds.

The rhythmic smack of the oars against the rippling water and the steady swish of the waves splashing over the prow were a monotonous music to Dean Jefferson's ears that did little to ease the growing tension in his mind. The swamplands in this godforsaken corner of Louisiana were places to be shunned at the best of times. He shifted his body uncomfortably on the hard seat of the tiny boat and turned once more to scrutinise the fellow who pulled on the oars, as though anxious to get him to the LaVey house as quickly as possible, and then beat it back to civilisation.

'I don't suppose you've any idea why Babette LaVey chose to live out here in the marshes?'

The boatman scowled, drawing his thin lips back across his jagged, splintered teeth. The action heightened the frightened look on his rugged features and threw into prominence the livid red scar that twisted down from below his left eye to just above his mouth. 'There ain't any way o' tellin' why anyone does these things,' he muttered. 'Maybe she was mad. Or if she wasn't then, she soon would be, livin' out here in the swamps.' He shrugged. 'How would I know? You'll have to ask her.' He spat over the side of the boat and gave an added heave on the oars.

'Didn't you know that she died a few days ago?'

The boatman looked genuinely surprised. His jaw dropped slackly open and he muttered something inaudible under his breath, then threw a startled glance at the darkness that stretched along the riverbank and pulled harder on the oars.

'No, I didn't know she was dead. But if it's true, there'll be bad times brewing in the swamps durin' the next few days.' He paused a moment, leaned forward in his seat, and allowed the boat to drift aimlessly with the current. His eyes lit up with an enigmatic wild gleam as he asked softly, 'Tell me, stranger, have they buried her yet? Or is she still lyin' there, up at the old mansion?'

Jefferson coughed. For a moment he was at a loss to know what to say. It was an unusual question for anyone to ask. Just what business was it of his? he thought angrily to himself. He opened his mouth to say some words of indignation, then bit them down. There was an expression on the other's dark face that he had never seen before. Fear and wonder and pleading were all blended together. It was obvious that the man was afraid of something. The anger subsided.

'Not that it's any business of yours, but she's still up at the LaVey place. Though I see no difference it can make whether she's still there or buried.'

The boatman regarded him in silence

for a long moment, then shook his head slowly. 'No, sir, I don't suppose you can. You've got no knowledge of these swamps. Things happen here that would seem impossible to the likes of you.'

Jefferson gave a snort of laughter. 'What are you talking about? Voodoo? Don't tell me that you believe in all that rot. You're letting your imagination run away with you.'

'Maybe.' The other swung the boat out of the main current and sent it spinning lazily across the thick oily water towards a narrow wooden jetty that had been erected on the edge of the river. 'But be that as it may, I wouldn't spend a single night in the LaVey place. No, sir. Not even for a couple of thousand dollars. And that's the truth.'

'Oh? What's wrong with the place? You think it's haunted, I suppose? Well, I'm a lawyer, and I deal only in practical matters. Facts are my business, not idle rumours.' Jefferson stepped from the boat and stood swaying momentarily on the platform of the jetty.

'You'll find the house at the end of the

pathway,' called the boatman as he lifted the lawyer's case from the boat and prepared to push off. 'But don't stray too far from the path. The swamps are mighty treacherous to those who don't know them.'

Jefferson pushed the dark thoughts that were whirling in his brain into the far background of his mind and watched the boat disappear into the shrouding mist, bobbing and side-slipping as the current caught it. The figure of the boatman in the stern was a hazy blur; a bloated shape that dipped and swayed in endless rhythm with the splashing oars. Squaring his shoulders, he stepped off the landing jetty onto the half-hidden pathway that snaked away between the straggling trees.

At thirty-nine, he was already near the top of his profession and comfortably off, with a flourishing practice in New Orleans. He grinned a little uneasily to himself in the darkness and pulled his thick coat tighter about his shoulders. What would his colleagues think if they could see him now, stumbling through mud that was almost ankle-deep, with the oozing, treacherous swamp on either side of the pathway and the grim forbidding spectre of a house that loomed in front of him?

His thoughts flashed back to the day five years earlier when he had first met Babette LaVey. Even then, she had seemed a peculiar character; glamorous, and with movie-star good looks — long black tresses framing an aristocratically shaped face, and a figure surpassing that of any woman he had met previously. He reckoned she was perhaps in her early forties. Yet there had been something about her; something undeniably alien, intangible, but nevertheless very real, that had set Jefferson on edge. But at that time, he hadn't been in a position to afford to be choosy about his clients. Besides, Babette LaVey was a widow who had money and an abundance of sex appeal; probably more than had been good for her. Even back then, rumour had it that she had travelled widely and had apparently dabbled in things that would have been best left alone.

She had seated herself in the chair in

front of Jefferson's desk, and leaned forward on her elbows in that unforgettably sensuous manner of hers, saying in a honeyed, seductive voice, 'I understand that you make a speciality of drawing up people's wills without asking too many awkward questions, Mr. Jefferson. I hope that my information has been correct, otherwise I'm wasting both your time and mine.'

'It's true enough,' Jefferson had admitted, loosening his collar a little. 'Though if there's anything crooked about it, I want no part of it. So tell me, just what is it you have in mind?'

'This,' Babette LaVey had said with a mesmerising smile, pushing a sheaf of papers over the desk towards him. 'My last will and testament. It may seem a little peculiar to you at first sight, but that's the way I want it, down to the last detail. I know what my relatives will try to do once I'm gone. They'll try to make out I was of unsound mind when it was drawn up. So there's five thousand dollars in addition to your normal fee if you make it as watertight as I've indicated. Do you think you can do it?'

Jefferson had taken the papers and read through them carefully, but as far as he had been able to see, there was nothing in it that violated the law. And although it was evident from the document that she was certainly peculiar, even eccentric, there was nothing there to show that her mind was affected. She had merely stipulated that for anyone to benefit under the terms of her will, they had to spend the night in her mansion in the swamplands. He had also to be present; and the will was not to be read, nor made public in any manner, until midnight on the third day following her death. There were various other small details that had to be approved, but as far as he could see, the only discomfort anyone would be asked to suffer would be the journey through the black swamps.

Dismissing the memory with a shake of his head, Jefferson pushed forward towards the looming shadow of the house, keeping his feet on the path that finally led him up to the wide sweep of the wooden veranda. Behind him, and on all sides, he could hear the occasional dull splash and the distant trilling of the whippoorwills. There was also an undeniable muted undertone of fear that was both capricious and deadly, menacing in its oddly persistent quality. He shivered in the cold night air and pulled savagely at the ancient bell-chain at the side of the door.

A bell chimed softly from somewhere deep inside the house. There followed a long moment of silence. Then, as Jefferson reached up to tug the chain again, he heard the unmistakable sound of footsteps, slow and halting, shuffling towards the door.

A chain rattled abruptly, and there was a sudden snap as a bolt was drawn aside. The door creaked open a little way, and a flood of yellow light spilled out on to the writhing mist.

'Yes? Who is it?' The voice was low and cracked and heavily accented.

Jefferson stepped forward a couple of paces and peered into the opening. Gradually, as his eyes adjusted, he was able to make out the dark shrivelled figure of an old brown-skinned Oriental, evidently a servant of some kind, staring back at him with wide, startled eyes. Briefly, he explained his presence.

The other scrutinised him for several moments, then opened the door wide. 'So you managed to get someone foolhardy enough to bring you out here after dark, eh? Well, well. Come in. Don't stand there in the mist.' Once Jefferson had entered, he slammed the door shut and slipped the bolt into place. 'If you'll come this way, sir, I'll take you to the library. We're still waiting for two more. But I don't expect they'll be long. They won't dawdle in the swamp. Not if they've any sense.' He led the way along a wide corridor.

The air in the house was cold and damp, and reeked of unplaceable odours that stung Jefferson's nostrils. Inside the library, however, there was a warm fire blazing in the open hearth and a hard, cheery brilliance that went most of the way towards dispelling the morbid fancies that whirled inside his brain.

A tall grey-haired dignified man in his early fifties was standing in front of the fire with his back to the flames. He strode forward to shake hands. 'The name's Martin Devlin. Glad you managed to get here,' he said genially. 'Don't know about you, but I had a hell of a job getting through those infernal swamps. At times I thought I was never going to make it. Couldn't get hold of a boat — or rather someone to ferry me out here — at any price. Finally managed to get one of the men to bring me out here, but he refused to wait to take me back, so I was forced to get Mason, the manservant, to put me up for the night. Can't say it's somewhere I'd willingly remain for the night if I had my choice in the matter.'

Jefferson grinned and nodded sympathetically, knowing something the other didn't. 'I agree.' He knew exactly how Devlin felt. He had the same feeling himself: a grim foreboding of evil that seemed to emanate from every corner of the house. It was as if the entire building itself was waiting, watchful and alert, holding them prisoners within its four walls until something utterly horrible happened. He shrugged the thought away and stepped closer to the fire to warm his hands. For the first time, he realised just how cold he really was.

The sound of voices came from a side room, and a door opened. A well-dressed couple entered the library. The man smiled welcomingly enough at Jefferson, but the look on the woman's face was one of deep suspicion.

'You must be the lawyer,' said the man. 'Pleased to meet you. I'm Brad Stevens and this is my wife, Annabelle.'

'Hello,' Jefferson replied. 'I was just saying to Mr. Devlin that I had a fairly easy journey here, but like you, the boatman refused to wait. I gather that this place isn't well liked in this district.'

'Well liked?' Annabelle barked a sudden laugh. 'You've got to be joking. Why, the place doesn't even have any electricity, just these old-fashioned oil lamps.' She gave a disparaging look around. 'It's beyond me how my sister ever managed to get that Mason fellow to stay here. My guess is that she picked him up abroad, for you wouldn't get any of the folk around here to stay in this house in the daytime, let alone at night.' A tall and

62

elegant brunette with a fleeting resemblance to her sibling, she took a sip from the wine glass she held. 'Besides, have you ever noticed how eerie the swamps are, especially now when it's dark? I felt it on the way here. I don't know exactly how to describe it. Almost as if I could see things, shapes, nothing more, vague and black and indistinct, slipping into view from behind us. Then, whenever I turned to look straight at them, they were gone.'

'Did you actually see anything?' asked Jefferson.

Annabelle gently bit her lower lip. Finally, she shook her head. 'No, nothing definite. Nothing I could swear to, anyway.'

Devlin leaned his tall body against the wall. 'Probably just your imagination.' He was about to add another comment when the front bell chimed.

They heard the shuffling of feet, followed by the clatter of the heavy bolt being withdrawn.

'No doubt that'll be Matilda and her son, the last of the beneficiaries,' muttered Stevens.

A moment later, the library door opened and the manservant ushered in Matilda LaVey — the deceased's aunt — and her son. She was small and thin. Her features were pale and pinched, the pallor of her narrow face accentuated somewhat by the abnormally high, prominent cheekbones. By contrast, Theodore LaVey was tall and vigorous, his broad features tanned brown with a life of prolonged exposure to the open air. He strode confidently into the room.

Jefferson noticed immediately that where his right arm should have been there was only an empty sleeve. Theodore LaVey noticed his glance. He grinned easily. 'Don't let that bother you,' he drawled loudly. 'Lost that up in Canada. Log fell on it over twenty years ago. Crushed it out of all recognition. Still, one good arm's better than none, that's what I always say.' He glanced round at his mother as if for confirmation.

'I take it you're the lawyer — Mr. Jefferson.' Something indefinable glinted in Matilda LaVey's eyes. 'I'm pleased to make your acquaintance. But now, if you don't mind, I'd be obliged if you would start with the reading of the will. There's no time like the present, and we're all here, aren't we?' She cast a somewhat disparaging look at the others before glancing back at Jefferson. 'I see we are. Then why are we wasting time?'

Jefferson motioned her to a seat at the table. It was time to get on with the proceedings. He waited until everyone had taken their places. 'Mrs. LaVey,' he said, opening by addressing the LaVey matriarch. 'Your late niece left certain instructions with me when she dictated the terms of her will five years ago.' He turned to face the others, noting the curious, expectant looks on their faces. 'One of them was that the reading of the will was not to take place until midnight three days after her death. I see that we still have forty minutes to wait. In the meantime, I suggest we get Mason to carry out certain other small details which were drawn up by Babette LaVey. Then we'll be ready to start.'

'Details!' Matilda LaVey sounded angry. 'What details?'

Jefferson shrugged his shoulders. 'You'll see what they are when we're ready,' he said quietly.

⋆　⋆　⋆

In the library, everything was quiet and still. Nothing seemed to move. The hands of the huge grandfather clock standing against the wall crept slowly until they stood almost at midnight.

Jefferson sat at the head of the long oaken table with the sealed envelope containing the will in front of him, reflecting on the utter strangeness of all this. There was no denying there was an element of the macabre about it, which made him feel uneasy. Sweat popped out on his forehead, and there was an unwelcome tingling sensation along his arms.

Matilda LaVey sat perched at the end; tight-lipped, obviously disapproving. Her son, Theodore, sat tall and straight in his chair beside her, a half-smile on his lips. Devlin was uneasy with the whole affair, and he was nervously toying with the cloth on the polished top. Brad and

Annabelle Stevens exchanged sly looks.

And at the far end of the room, stiff and cold, Babette LaVey lay in her coffin, the heavy lid open, according to her last wish, her eyes staring mockingly and sightlessly at the low ceiling. The only light in the room apart from the feeble glow from the dying embers in the hearth came from the five tall, slim candles set in solid silver sticks in the middle of the table.

In spite of the tight grip he was holding on himself, Jefferson jerked upright instinctively in his chair as the first dull chime of midnight boomed from the interior of the clock. He took a deep breath. 'I can now begin the reading of the will.' Carefully, he slit the slim envelope he had brought with him along one edge with a letter-opener and took out the last will and testament of Babette LaVey.

Annabelle coughed nervously from the other end of the table and threw an apprehensive glance towards the long shape of the coffin that rested against the wall at the end of the room. Beneath the table, she shuffled her feet softly, but the noise seemed oddly magnified in the silence of the room.

Jefferson cleared his throat. The papers crackled dryly as he opened the will and spread it out flat on the table in front of him. Putting on his spectacles, he began to read it. 'The terms of the will are very simple,' he announced. 'Babette LaVey, although some of you may not have realised it before, was a very wealthy woman. The estate is worth almost three million dollars. This is to be divided equally among as many beneficiaries as are present at the reading and are still in the house, *alive*, on the morning of the following day. All the books in the library, including any personal documents, are left to Mason, in recognition of his unfailing loyalty throughout their many years together. There are in addition a few small legacies to various institutions, but I will deal with these personally upon my return to New Orleans.' He leaned back in his chair. 'Well, that's all. Now, are there any questions?'

'Yes! What exactly did she mean by

saying those who are still here, *alive*, by the following morning?' snapped Matilda. 'Did she expect us to leave — or die in our beds from the shock of such sudden generosity?'

'I'm afraid I've no idea what was in your late niece's mind when she inserted that clause into the will.'

'I don't see what we're all arguing about,' commented Stevens. 'None of us are in a position to leave tonight, unless we decide to jump into the river and swim back to town. And I, for one, don't fancy that. Besides, surely it isn't too much for us to humour Babette, especially when we're each getting several hundred thousand dollars into the bargain.'

Jefferson opened his mouth to say something in support of this view, however avaricious it may have seemed, but the words were never said.

There was a sudden, unexpected movement.

Annabelle was on her feet, her face twisted in horror. Her chair fell to the floor behind her, knocked over by the abrupt movement. She screamed and pointed a trembling finger at the coffin, which lay just inside the rim of light thrown by the flickering candles.

Jefferson half-rose to his feet, then stopped as if struck, both physically and mentally. He felt his stomach churn as sudden terror crowded all other thoughts out of his mind, threatening to overwhelm him completely.

Flicking a slime-coated forked tongue, a hideous sharp-clawed grey lizard, a foot in length, clambered slowly over the edge of the coffin — a grotesque shape that dropped down with a soft thud on to the floor. Swiftly, it scuttled across the room and vanished from sight beneath the heavy silken curtains covering the open doorway which led to the hall.

It was several seconds before anyone moved.

Then Devlin, who was nearest to the coffin, stepped cautiously forward and peered inside. Drunkenly, he staggered back. When he looked round again, his face was ashen. He lurched to one side and began to gag. Vomit leaked from between the fingers clamped to his mouth.

70

'In God's name, what is it?' cried Jefferson.

Devlin could only retch and point at the coffin.

Steeling himself, Jefferson went over and looked inside.

There was a gaping bloody hole in Babette LaVey's abdomen from which a greenish bilious ichor leaked. Pieces of broken eggshell lay inside. Either the lizard had somehow got in unnoticed and had begun to gorge itself on her corpse, or it had emerged from that gruesome cavity; an abominable birth which had spawned something truly monstrous.

Everyone was on their feet now, most of them having retreated away from the curtained exit.

Stevens edged his way to the coffin to look inside. 'Jesus, that's disgusting!' His voice sounded strangely like a sob. 'None of you ladies should come up here. Stay back!' he cautioned, his voice grim.

Devlin looked across at Jefferson. His mouth was twisting madly. He drew himself up. 'What the hell? It's all some ghastly trick. It's got to be,' he said

71

loudly. Wiping the spittle from his mouth, he came up for a second look as though to prove to himself that this was no grisly illusion. The sight repulsed him. Fighting back his revulsion, he leant against the coffin and shook his head disbelievingly.

'What's happened?' asked Annabelle, her voice weak and wavering.

'You don't want to know.' Stevens lowered the coffin lid. 'It's not pretty.'

Jefferson stared about, seeing if he could detect that horrible lizard. Like the others, he was scared and utterly bewildered. Something had to be done, and it had to be done quickly, before things developed into full-blown terror and panic. Otherwise, there would be no way of telling what the consequences would be.

'My guess is this is all part of some conspiracy — some trick to try and scare us away so that we're not entitled to our share of the estate,' said Annabelle. 'One of the 'details' Mason had to take care of. My bitch of a sister would've found this funny.'

Jefferson raised a trembling hand, glancing uneasily around. 'Please, take my word for it. I'm as confused as you are. Believe me, there was nothing relating to this in her instructions.' There was no sign of the loathsome creature that had crawled out of the coffin. But he had the feeling that it was still somewhere around, watching their every move from some unlit corner, lurking beneath the folds of the heavy curtains.

Devlin had armed himself with the poker. 'I guess that thing must've come from the swamp. Let's hope that's where it's gone.'

'It didn't look like any 'gator I've ever seen before,' said Stevens. 'And me and Annabelle live down in Florida on the edge of the Everglades where there's hundreds of them.'

'Well be that as it may, I suggest that when we go to bed, we all lock our doors,' said Devlin gravely. 'If there is anything on the prowl, we might as well take the proper precautions.'

'Personally, I don't think it's anything to get too alarmed about.' Jefferson sounded like he was trying to convince himself.

Theodore scraped back his chair and got to his feet. 'I think I'll go for a breath of fresh air before turning in. The mist seems to have cleared away a little now. Besides, there's something about this house that I don't like.'

'Suit yourself, but I'm going to turn in for the night, though God knows whether I'll get any sleep. I don't mind telling you all that this place gives me the creeps.' Devlin rose from his chair.

'I doubt whether any of us will get much sleep this night,' muttered Annabelle.

'All I'm waiting for is tomorrow morning, so that I can get away from this damned place as soon as possible,' said Devlin, heading for the door.

'I think that goes for all of us.' Theodore let himself out through the French windows and closed them softly behind him. He stalked away in the moonlight towards the sluggish waters of the swamp.

★ ★ ★

Half an hour later, when Theodore hadn't returned, Jefferson and Stevens went out to look for him. The air outside was cold and still, like an invisible cloak of death that hung unmoving, over the house. The moon was still up, shining white, like a disc of frozen fire between the rubbery leaves, providing them with sufficient light by which to see.

LaVey hadn't got far. They found his corpse sprawled face downwards less than a hundred yards from the house.

'Christ! This is all we need. We'd better take a look at him before we carry him back to the house,' said Jefferson in a low murmur. His voice made an uneasy sound in the blend of night noises. 'It would be foolish to upset the others, especially the women, if it's nothing more than a heart attack.'

'Heart attack?' Stevens sounded surprised. 'Why man, he might only have had one arm, but he was as strong and as healthy as an ox. That wasn't what killed him.' He got his hand beneath the body and rolled it over onto its back, uttering a startled gasp as a heap of bloody, steaming entrails slid from the dead man's torn open abdomen. The corpse had been ripped to shreds by some devilish, savage fury. The eyes, wide and staring, were filled with a horror beyond life, gazing sightlessly at the white moon. 'God . . . I think I'm going to be sick.'

'Let's . . . let's get him up to the house,' muttered Jefferson. 'There's nothing more we can do here, except possibly run into the monster that killed him. Possibly it was an alligator that got him. There's bound to be a few running loose around here. He must have known it was dangerous to come out into the swamp.' He bent to lift the dead man's solitary hand.

'Is that a gun lying there?' queried the other, wiping spittle from his chin.

'Yes, I believe it is.' Jefferson stooped and picked up the heavy revolver, which lay half-hidden in the grass a couple of inches from the mangled man's out-stretched hand. He held it up in the moonlight. With a nervous expertise, he flipped the chamber open experimentally and examined it carefully. He sniffed the end of the barrel. 'It hasn't been fired. As for why he never cried out, well — your guess is as good as mine. Maybe whatever did this surprised him. Came at him from behind, perhaps.' He stuffed the gun into the pocket of his coat and caught hold of the dead man by the shoulders. 'You take his feet and we'll get him into the house. We should put a call through to the local police. At least one thing's certain, we won't need a doctor for him. God knows how the old woman's going to take it.'

Together, they carried the ravaged body back into the house.

Mason and Annabelle met them in the entrance.

'Have you found any sign yet of — Oh!' Annabelle started forward.

Behind her, Jefferson caught a glimpse of Matilda. 'You'd better stay where you are, Mrs. LaVey,' he called urgently. 'There's been an accident. I'm afraid your son's been killed. There's nothing anyone can do for him.'

The old woman was having none of it. She rushed forward as fast as she could and tried to grab her dead son. Wailing her grief, she slumped to the floor, tears streaming down her lined face, collecting in the furrows of her skin.

Annabelle tried to calm her down. Grabbing her by her skinny arms, she managed to steer the other away into the lounge.

Alerted by the mournful cries, Devlin came bounding down the stairs.

'Mason, is there a telephone in the house?' Jefferson asked.

'No, I'm afraid not.'

Jefferson cursed. His mind was swimming and his hands, shirt and trousers were covered in blood. Briefly he explained everything to Devlin.

The other listened patiently until he was finished. Then he said thinly, 'Do you think it was an alligator? Because I don't.'

'What other explanation is there?' replied Jefferson.

'Hell, I don't know,' Stevens said angrily. 'Ever since I entered this house earlier tonight, I've had the feeling that there's something evil and malignant here. I've tried to shake it off, but it's impossible. It isn't just the swamps and the talk I heard on the way here. It's something more than that. Something terribly real.'

Jefferson examined the blood on his hands. 'It would be best not to repeat any of this in front of Mrs. LaVey or your wife. Once we get out of here, we can let the police deal with it. Until then, we've got to go on the assumption that there's a wild animal on the loose outside. And the sooner we do something about it, the better. Don't you agree?'

'But what makes more sense — going outside and hunting this thing or waiting here for it to strike again, if indeed it does? If it is an alligator, then I can't see it entering the house. Theodore was unfortunate but these things happen in the swamps. If you want my opinion, we should stay inside; lock all the doors and secure all the windows,' said Devlin.

'I feel somewhat uncomfortable mentioning this; but do you think Theodore was killed by that creature which crawled out of Babette's coffin?' queried Stevens.

'It's possible, I guess,' reasoned Jefferson. 'But that thing was small. I'd have thought that whatever killed him was substantially bigger, much bigger.' He stared at the gun in his hand. 'Whether it'll strike again, I don't know; but contrary to your recommendation, Mr. Devlin, I think it'd be best if we take a look outside. Make sure it's not lurking around the house. With a few shots we should be able to kill it or at the very least drive it way. The last thing we want is for it to get in somehow and kill us while we're sleeping. There's bound to be some more weapons around the house somewhere. Let's take a look.'

★   ★   ★

For twenty minutes, the three men scouted around the bushes and undergrowth that fronted the river without seeing the slightest sign of anything untoward. They took it in turns to keep watch on the house, to see that the lights were still burning in the bedroom windows. Jefferson carried the gun he had found close to Theodore's eviscerated corpse. Stevens had an old rifle which, although serviceable, had clearly seen better days, whilst Devlin had armed himself with the poker and a large carving knife which he had found in the kitchen.

All the time they stepped softly and carefully, keeping their weapons at the ready. But at first there was nothing. Only the low sibilant murmur of the wind in the branches and the steady slap of the water lapping against the jetty.

'Doesn't look as though there's anything here,' said Stevens. 'Maybe we'd do better if we spread out a little, instead of sticking together.'

'If you think that'd be best,' muttered Jefferson. 'But don't go wandering off too far on your own. Remember what happened to LaVey.'

Stevens stalked off through the low-hanging branches of the surrounding trees. For a long moment, Jefferson could hear his footsteps growing fainter and fainter. Then there was silence.

'I only hope he knows what he's doing,' said Devlin. 'If you ask me, he's just asking for trouble.'

A long moment passed. Then they heard a cry from over on their right. An instant later, there came the unmistakable sound of a rifle shot. It was followed quickly by another. And then another.

Devlin's fingers closed tightly on Jefferson's arm, biting into the flesh with a steel-like grip. 'Something's happened,' he yelled harshly. 'It came from that direction. Come on.'

Together, they scrambled through the watery undergrowth. This time they made no effort to move quietly. Speed was the only thing they were interested in.

It was Devlin who stumbled into the marshy clearing first. 'Jesus!' he said thickly. 'What is it?'

Jefferson stared over the other's shoulder. What he saw sickened him.

Stevens lay twisted on the smooth earth, his body contorted, arms outstretched, his feet hunched up beneath him. His head had been wrenched from his shoulders and was now in the clawed hand of the thing that was illuminated in the hideous yellow moonlight, standing over him — a huge upright reptilian abomination, eight feet or so in height, its wide-open jaws wet and slimy and dripping. Much of its scaly body was hidden by the tall reeds which grew right up to the riverbank, but its long evil-looking snout was sticking out from among the shadows.

Jefferson lifted his gun and squeezed the trigger twice. The bullets struck the monster's pale, ribbed underbelly.

It lifted its head and stood poised over the headless corpse, obviously deliberating whether to attack the new intruders or retreat into the river. Slavering a bloody drool, it beat its ridged tail into the mire before slipping back among the reeds. There was a splash and a rippling of waves across the smooth surface of the river.

'Bastard's got clean away,' muttered Jefferson, walking to the water's edge and peering along the clear stretch of the river. 'There's no sign of it now. But I'm sure I hit it. It was impossible to miss at that distance.' He went down towards the river and bent on one knee, battling to come to terms with all he had seen. His thoughts stopped abruptly at a sudden startled cry from his companion. Madly, he leapt to his feet. There was a long rippling swish and a line of white foam on the water where the river was running in the shallows like a line of spilled ink. Desperately, he heaved himself forward, shouting a vague warning. But he was too late.

Devlin toppled forward on his face in the water. There was the drag and scuffle of something big, lumbering and heaving itself out of the swamp. A spray of crimson arced into the air.

A red mist seemed to float in front of Jefferson's eyes and a wave of nausea threatened to overwhelm him. When finally he was able to see clearly again, Devlin was gone and there was the huge shape of the monstrous lizard lifting itself out of the sluggish waters of the river, coming towards him through the swaying reeds, a severed arm falling from its blood filled jaws. Closer it came, and closer, until he could see the full size of it, and the malignant gleam of its wicked eyes. Hell glared briefly at him. Moonlight shone wetly on its claws and scales.

Frantically, Jefferson raised his gun and squeezed the trigger until the hammer clicked dully on an empty chamber. Still the creature came on. Wildly, he turned and ran, tripping over bushes and roots in his headlong flight, not caring about anything except to get back to the house. Behind him, he could hear the muffled squelching of the creature's feet in the ooze as it ploughed its way after him.

Only when he reached the house did he stop running and throw a frightened glance over his shoulder. But the monster had disappeared somewhere in the darkness of the swamp. He stood still for a moment, in absolute silence. Even the dull rippling of the oily water seemed to have stopped.

Panting heavily, he stepped inside the house and slammed the door hard behind him, hurriedly throwing the bolt into place. The muscles of his stomach twisted themselves into a tight knot of fear. Without pausing, he rushed into the silent library, with the coffin still lying where it had been left at the end of the room and stared at the candles on the oaken table.

Three of them were now out.

Creeping shadows drifted out of the lightless corners as the darkness increased. For the first time, he fully accepted that he was up against something supernatural — that the horror that was responsible for the deaths of three men was no normal creature. The sudden shock of the realisation hit him like a physical blow. He reached out and grasped the table for support. Turning swiftly on his heel, he ran out of the room, up the wide stairway, and onto the landing at the top. Urgently, he rapped on the door of the nearest bedroom.

A moment later, Annabelle's voice reached him. She was obviously still wide awake. 'Who is it?' She came to the door and opened it slightly, then further as she saw who it was. 'Oh, Mr. Jefferson. It's you. Did you find anything? Or probably — ' Her voice trailed away into silence. She put her hand to her mouth. 'Something's happened,' she cried thinly.

Jefferson nodded dumbly. 'I'm afraid so,' he said softly. 'Martin and Brad are dead. There was nothing anyone could do. We're up against something here that not even bullets can harm. In fact, I doubt whether we'll even be safe in our rooms, with the doors locked. The only sure way is for us to get away from here as soon as possible. At once if we can.'

'Brad's . . . Brad's dead?'

Jefferson grabbed her around the shoulders and stared hard into her eyes. 'We have to get out of here.' She went slack in his arms and he was afraid that she was going to faint, but with a sudden conscious effort she pulled herself together and took a tight grip on herself. 'Have you seen Mason?' he asked.

Her eyes watering, Annabelle shook her head.

'It might be for the best if you — '

There came a sudden loud crash as of a window being broken, followed by a woman's scream from a room further along the landing.

'What now?' Relinquishing his hold on Annabelle, Jefferson cautiously made his way along the corridor, his gun held out before him. There were dreadful noises coming from inside Matilda LaVey's bedroom; it sounded as though a pride of hungry lions had been released inside.

'Oh my God! What is it?' asked Annabelle, edging her way forward.

Jefferson shook his head. They stood looking at each other, scared almost to the point of paralysis for the best part of a minute — until the sounds had stopped. Unsure as to whether he was doing the right thing, he reached out and gingerly tried the handle. The door was locked. 'Stand back. There's just a chance we may be in time.' Madly, he threw his entire weight at the door. At first, it refused to move an inch. On his second attempt, there was a sudden shriek of tortured metal and the lock burst open with a sudden snap that threw him into the room. Desperately, he struggled to retain his balance. Cold air from the large smashed windows directly opposite gusted inside.

'Oh my God! Aunt Matilda!' Annabelle gave a stifled scream and pointed.

Matilda LaVey lay torn and mangled on the floor. Her head dangled by a stretch of bloody gristle and one of her legs had been torn from her body. Her tongue lolled stupidly from between her lips. A huge pool of blood covered the carpet.

Jefferson had seen enough. His mind reeling from the gruesome discovery, he grabbed Annabelle by the arm and steered her outside. 'Our only chance is to find a boat. There has to be one someplace. Otherwise, how did LaVey get into town?'

'I hadn't thought of that. But what if that thing's waiting for us, out there in the swamp? We'd never stand a chance.'

'Maybe. But that's a risk we'll have to take. It's better than sitting here and waiting for it to come to us.'

'You're right,' she muttered. 'Let's get out of this place before we're both killed.'

Together, they made their way down the winding stairway and along the narrow passageway at the bottom. There was no sign of the manservant and the lawn outside seemed deserted in the pale moonlight.

Five minutes later, they found a tiny boat moored a couple of feet from the edge of the jetty, almost completely hidden among the reeds.

Jefferson pulled it out with a sudden, shoulder-wrenching heave. 'Get in,' he said sharply. 'The sooner we're away from here the better.' He glanced up quickly at a sudden scream from Annabelle. Her eyes were wide and she was pointing a shaking finger over his shoulder. With a sudden instinctive movement, he whirled and stared back towards the house. From out of the corner of his eye, he glimpsed the dark shape that rushed down on him from out of the liquid moonlight. The next instant the thing was on him, its weight thrusting down on his shoulders forcing him to the soggy ground. Madly, he strove to remain upright, pulling the gun from his pocket and fired three bullets. The creature smelt musty and reeked of sulphur, death and decay. And there was a vacant, dead expression in the red-rimmed eyes that contrasted strangely with the fierce expression on the grinning features.

Jaws like a bear trap and serrated teeth that could shred a man to the bone in a single bite reached down for his unprotected throat. Desperately, he tried to get his feet beneath him, to push himself upright. But it was no use. A filthy claw raked across his ribs, lacerating his shirt. Four parallel wounds filled instantly with blood. With a hiss, its serpent-like tongue flicked before his eyes. His gun was sent spiralling to the mud.

Suddenly a voice called out, the words strange and foreign. The horror barged Jefferson to the ground and lumbered back before dropping to all four stumpy feet.

Grinning wickedly, Mason stepped from the shadows. He raised an arm and pointed at Annabelle, who was still in the small boat. Painfully, Jefferson could only watch from where he lay as the huge reptile, now eleven or so feet in length, began to pound towards the woman.

With a scream, Annabelle pulled on the paddles, rowing the boat out into the water. The monster slinked into the morass, disappearing from sight. Thrashing its tail, it surfaced a moment later, knocking into the boat, overturning it.

Splashing, Annabelle tried to make her way to the water's edge, but to no avail. Struggling frantically, she was dragged under. Somehow, she fought her way to the surface and began swimming for the nearest bank. Clawing feebly at the mud, her slender hands tearing huge clumps of glistening weed, she was hauled back, vanishing into the muddy depths. A pool of darkened crimson spread out.

Mason's grin widened. He walked over to where Jefferson lay, bleeding and wounded. 'And that . . . as they say, is that.'

'What . . . are you talking about?' Jefferson began to shiver. There was blood leaking from him. He couldn't feel his legs and he was convinced he was dying. The pain from the slash he had received across his ribs was excruciating. Blood streamed down the side of his face.

'First, let's get you inside.' Mason crouched and assisted the injured lawyer, getting him to his feet.

Had he been at full strength, Jefferson would have seriously considered throttling the old man, but instead he let himself be helped back towards the house, reasoning that the last thing he wanted was for that hellish lizard to return. His mind was hazy. Had the manservant somehow called it off only to then send it against Annabelle as though it were a trained pet? Was such a thing possible? Limping inside, supported by the other, the crazy notion that all of this was just some kind of a protracted nightmare struck him. He was only vaguely aware of entering the library and being lowered into a chair.

Now that all of the candles were out, Mason lit a gas lamp and placed it on the table. He then went into the kitchen, returning with a bowl of water and a strip of bandages. 'If you want to live, sit still while I treat your wound.' Opening the other's shirt, he began cleaning the nasty-looking claw marks, applying a brown liquid that stung like hell. 'If you're lucky, this will prevent any infection,' he said.

Jefferson winced but said nothing, surrendering himself to the other's ministrations.

'Sit up whilst I strap this bandage in place.'

With some difficulty, the lawyer did as he was told. Breathing was painful.

'Now then, you and I have some talking to do.' Briefly appraising his life-saving first aid, Mason stepped back. 'Would you care for a little drink?'

Jefferson shook his head.

'Very well.' Mason sat down, elbows on the table, fingers interlinked. His attitude had become business-like. 'My real name is Zulfikar Leng, and I am a descendant of the Indonesian Bugis people of Flores. My ancestors were worshippers of the Komodo — the lizard, or rather monitor, you've seen tonight.' He gestured towards the window.

Jefferson followed the movement and saw to his horror the slavering, saurian snout pressed up against the glass. He shuddered, causing a sharp pain to lance through his chest. Even if he could overpower the manservant, there would be no escape.

'I first met the recently widowed Babette LaVey some twenty years ago when she visited Banu Nggulung to learn for herself the truth about the mighty 'dragons'. She became very interested in my beliefs, so much so that when she returned to America she brought me with her, eager to learn more. I taught her the ancient ceremonies, the spells and the means of spiritually becoming one with the Komodo. From a willing neophyte, in time, she became a high priestess, capable of the transformation.'

Jefferson listened, his face creased in a frown of incredulity and fear.

'An extraordinarily spiteful woman, when she found out that she was dying, she pleaded with me to devise a plan which would enable her to get her revenge on her relatives from beyond the grave. She told me that they had all had a hand in killing her husband. And so . . . it was agreed that on the day of her death I would perform the ritual, the sorcery, which would permit her to give life, even in the midst of death, to the Komodo.'

Had he not witnessed these horrible events for himself, Jefferson would have sworn that the old man was insane.

Instead, he sagged in his chair, succumbing to the pain in his body and the madness of it all. 'Why keep me alive then?' There were so many unanswered questions but for now this one was the most pressing.

'Why?' Nonchalantly, the manservant scraped away a small piece of dirt from a fingernail. 'You've done her no wrong. Besides . . . I have a problem. I understand I am officially the heir to Babette's estate — I was there at the reading of the will, in the shadows, admittedly, but there all the same; and I'm the only one alive now. Is this correct?'

Jefferson thought of the terms of the will and nodded.

'Good. However, the disappearance of all of the other heirs is bound to raise questions.' He leant forward and fixed the lawyer with an unblinking gaze. 'All I want is this house and enough money to last me until my death. I'm prepared to split the estate with you, fifty-fifty, if you'll say that the others never turned up; and I can assure you the bodies will never be found. I can pay off the boatmen easily enough, one way or another.'

Jefferson struggled to form a response, such was the turmoil in his mind. 'So . . . this was all done to get at the money?'

'That . . . and revenge. So, what's your decision? Will you assist me and make yourself considerably richer, or . . . ' The sentence was left hanging.

Aware that the consequence of not agreeing to the scheme would almost certainly be a grisly death, either here or wherever else this sorcerer's power could reach, Jefferson weakly extended a muddy, blood-covered hand. 'All right. I'll do it.' He had made several morally dubious decisions during the course of his career; but as he sealed this unholy agreement, he felt as though part of his soul was being torn away as assuredly as his body would be torn to pieces if he were to refuse.

FOREIGN BODIES

The best defence is a strong offence.

'Hell, I never thought I'd hear myself say this but I'm with the Chinese on this one.' Colonel Frank 'Gunner' Kennington of the U.S. Marine Corp. stared at the large screen, watching the live subtitled updates that were being broadcast direct from the U.N. Headquarters.

Yet another emergency meeting of the Security Council had been arranged, and the Chinese ambassador had once again vociferously called for an immediate air strike on the off-sea Douglas-McKray exploratory drilling platform which lay some thirty miles off the Ecuadorian coast. Both the Russians and the French were coming around to his proposal.

'You know as well as I do that our government would never authorise such action while we're still receiving transmissions. Admittedly they're becoming weaker, and

God knows how anyone can still be — '
First Lieutenant Bill Henderson stopped
abruptly as the images of the diplomatic
arena changed and images of the drilling
platform — or rather what it had now
become — appeared on the screen.

The footage, taken from the relative
safety of a circling news helicopter, showed
the huge rig encased within a weird blue-
green frogspawn-like jelly. The camera zoomed
in on the surface, and it was possible to
make out various structures underneath
the thick semi-transparent membranous
coating.

'You know, nine years ago the world
held its breath worrying whether Kennedy
and Khrushchev were going to blast us all
back to the Stone Age,' commented Kennington. 'Three years ago the world watched
in awe as Armstrong stepped out on to
the surface of the moon. Less than a year
later, millions sat glued to their televisions
praying for a miracle aboard Apollo Thirteen. Now this . . . whatever the hell it is,
is on every TV in every country.'

'To be honest with you, I'm surprised
that our government decided to go public

with it,' Henderson replied.

'News would've leaked out sooner or later. This wasn't something that could've been covered up like all the other stuff we can't talk about.' Kennington sat back in his chair as the delegates at the U.N. Headquarters reappeared on the screen. 'The thing now is how to deal with it. I think we can expect to get the call very soon.'

'So you really think that we'll be asked to investigate?'

Kennington grinned. 'It's what we do, isn't it?'

★　★　★

Fourteen hours later, Kennington, Henderson and a dozen hand-picked heavily armed marines stepped from the U.S. air force military plane on to the landing strip at Manta. The flight from Fort Bragg, North Carolina had gone without incident, although everyone aboard the aircraft knew that this was far from a routine mission. It had now been three days since the first emergency call from the drilling platform had alerted the Ecuadorian coastguard to something strange happening, and over ten hours since all contact had been lost.

An Ecuadorian military official who introduced himself as Colonel Edgardo Paz greeted them on the runway, ushering them towards a nearby hangar. Once they had all assembled inside, he led Kennington and Henderson to a side office whilst the marines set about checking their equipment. There were two other men in the office — a short, plump, bespectacled man with a balding head, and a young Japanese man.

'May I introduce Professor Gleeson of the marine biological institute based in Quito, and Doctor Yang-Si of the seismological team here in Manta,' said Paz. 'Both will be accompanying you.'

Kennington gave a brusque nod, the limit of his greeting. He was the one in charge, and it was important that the others knew this as well. 'So, have there been any other developments since we lost contact with the Douglas-McKray?'

'None whatsoever,' answered Gleeson.

'However, the latest film images taken from one of the survey helicopters seems to suggest a change in the *constituency* of the substance which has formed over the rig.'

'A change? What sort of change?' inquired Kennington.

Gleeson removed his glasses and gave them a clean. 'Well, from a purely visual perspective, it would appear that the coating has hardened, altering from a semi-liquid to one which appears more solid. Indeed, portions of it have now coalesced into denser segments. It's hard to say whether such a solidification is a result of time or a reaction to air or sunlight.'

Kennington's steely gaze hardened. As a man of action, he had little patience for academics. As far as he was concerned, the likelihood of there being any survivors out there on that rig was now negligible; and thus the sooner it was sent to the bottom of the sea, with whatever weird contagion had spread over it, the better. It seemed to him unnecessarily dangerous to lead a detachment of his men and these two 'eggheads' out there to discover just what was going on, and yet those were his orders. 'You're the experts. What's your explanation for this?' he asked.

'As representatives of the scientific community, we're as baffled as you are,' replied Gleeson. 'This is completely unprecedented. Not until we obtain a sample of whatever that substance is for analysis can we begin to formulate a hypothesis. However, Doctor Yang-Si believes that it may in some way be linked to recent tectonic movements on the seabed.' He gestured to his colleague.

'That is correct,' Yang-Si affirmed. 'At this stage it is but a theory. There have been slight, yet observable, seismological movements along the seabed in the vicinity of the drilling platform. The fault line between the Nazca and the South American Plates lies less than a thousand kilometres from where some of the investigatory boring was performed. It's possible that in the drilling process a substratum reservoir of an as yet unidentified mineral has been tapped, resulting in an immense chemical reaction the oxidisation effects of which are plainly visible.'

'I was of the understanding that this was a living organism,' countered Kennington. 'If I get you right, you're suggesting that it's some kind of chemical. Something like tar thickening on a road?'

'That is my belief.' Yang-Si nodded. 'However, as Professor Gleeson has said, not until we can analyse it can we reach an accurate decision.'

'What about survival chances? Do you think anyone could still be alive out there?' As far as Kennington was concerned, this was the fundamental question.

Gleeson rubbed his chin thoughtfully. 'I'd think it unlikely. Given that this substance seems to have completely smothered the exterior of the rig, I think we have to go on the assumption that it has leaked into the interior as well. There may well be pockets free from its contamination but of course we have no idea as to whether or not there are any other biological hazards to be on the lookout for; gaseous emissions, toxicity levels and of course radiation.'

'You think it may be radioactive in origin?' asked Henderson from where he stood near the door.

'It's possible, although readings thus far obtained have indicated only ambient levels,' answered Gleeson. 'However, we've no way of knowing what it's like inside. Which is all the more reason to go out there and find out.'

* * *

Despite having seen and experienced many things over the course of his highly decorated military career, Kennington found it hard to fully take in the enormity and the sheer alienness of the sight visible through the porthole windows of the military helicopter. Even from this distance, he could see that the entire structure was cocooned in a weird crystalline crust which extended all the way from the uppermost buildings down to the very sea level — and perhaps deeper. The fact that none of the rig's personnel had managed to escape via the emergency helicopter suggested to him that whatever had occurred here had been both swift and merciless — the initial encasement within the more gelatinous matter perhaps occurring in one monumental, disastrous, geyser-like upsurge. Such a view strengthened the opinion that in the course of the investigatory boring some subterranean reservoir had been punctured resulting in a high pressure release. The thought made him think of the pictures of gushing Texan oil wells he had seen.

'It's like something out of *The Blob*! It's ... bloody unreal,' commented Henderson. Like Kennington, he too had his eyes fixed on the befouled edifice.

'It's real all right.' Kennington turned to face the gathered marines, all of them dressed in their chemical and biological protective suits. 'Once we get aboard, we stick to the plan. For now, this is a search and rescue mission. I don't want any heroics.'

The helicopter banked slightly, righted itself and began to hover, the almost deafening sound of the rotor blades drowning out all other noise. A door was opened and a gust of foul-smelling air blasted inside.

Kennington looked down. Thirty feet below him, he could see the dark green and glistening surface. It looked like a kind of strange algae. Some parts were mottled a disgusting, dark, watery red, giving it the obscene appearance of blood-streaked catarrh which had somehow coagulated into a dense crust.

The first of the marines, a Vietnam veteran named Max Wilbur, clipped himself onto the line and with a final nod to his commanding officer abseiled down, his bulky protective suit impeding his progress. Kennington watched him go, half-expecting to see his man sink into the hellish depths of the unearthly surface; but to his relief, the other did nothing of the sort. With a thumbs-up, Wilbur unbuckled himself from the line and stomped down hard with a boot, signalling to Kennington that the surface was solid.

Over the course of the next ten minutes, the rest of the team lowered themselves from the helicopter. Like astronauts on a foreign planet, some began taking readings and samples from the surrounding biosphere; the air was sampled and, with the use of geologists' hammers, chippings and portions of the bizarre crust were collected and bagged.

Having come to the realisation that his surroundings posed no immediate biohazard, Kennington lowered his face mask and went over to where Gleeson was eagerly conducting a few mineralogical tests. 'Well, what have we got here?' he asked.

The chubby marine biologist removed his face-piece. 'I'm not sure. It's definitely organic. High levels of iron with numerous terrestrial trace elements, so I think we can safely rule out anything from another planet.'

Kennington nodded. 'Any idea how thick it is?'

'It varies. Initial probing suggests between six and ten feet.'

'Right. Let's see about drilling through this stuff.'

Equipment and boring apparatus was lowered from the helicopter and soon a team of marines set to excavating through the strange coating. It proved to be a lengthy and difficult process, the solidity varying between rock-hard and gelatinous with each foot they delved. After twenty minutes, a slime-covered aperture wide enough for a man had been tunnelled, at the bottom of which could be seen a metallic surface.

'Going by the map, I'd say that's the top of the main canteen,' said Kennington, peering down the hole. 'If we drill through, we should be able to create an access point.'

Dutifully, two of his team set to the task. The space was widened and a remote surveillance camera was lowered. A technician hooked it up to a portable monitor, and Kennington and the scientists looked on apprehensively as images of the deserted canteen appeared on the screen. There were no signs of life . . . nor were there any bodies. Everything was still.

'There could be anything down there,' muttered Gleeson.

Kennington snorted. 'I'm going down. I want Henderson, Wilbur and three others. The rest of you stay up here and remain in contact at all times.'

'I plan on accompanying you,' said Gleeson a little reluctantly. 'No disrespect, Colonel, but it might do to have a little brains in the expedition. Besides, I may be able to get some better samples — discover just what this stuff is and find out what caused it.'

'Okay, Professor, but let's get one thing straight. This isn't *Star Trek*. I'm not Captain Kirk, my men aren't expendable red-shirts, and you're not Spock. We take this nice and easy.'

★　★　★

A chill dankness hung over everything, yet the air was breathable, although some men chose to wear their masks as a precautionary measure.

It came as no surprise to find that the electrics were out. Consequently, three of the seven carried high-powered flashlights. The shadows danced strangely as they panned their light sources around the walls and countless surfaces. Darkened, obscured windows reflected the light back, enabling them to discern that they were now effectively cocooned.

Noting the multiple exits leading from the room, Kennington assessed the situation. 'Okay. Two groups. Gleeson and Wilbur, you're with me. Henderson, you take control of the others. Check out the main mess hall on the level below this one and the sleeping dorms.' He looked at his watch. 'We meet back here in thirty minutes. Then, if we find no survivors, we get the hell out of here and send this rig to the bottom of the sea. Check in every five minutes on the radio.' Henderson nodded, gathered his marines together and set off for a darkened opening on the far side.

Once they had disappeared from view, Kennington led the two who were accompanying him in the opposite direction. Shadows seemed to flow and shift as they progressed through the labyrinth of dark rooms and corridors, their footsteps echoing disturbingly. A network of massive flanged and riveted pipes twisted their way throughout the structure. They soon came to a metal stairway that descended into the inky depths.

'Strange that we've yet to find a body,' commented Gleeson.

'Could be that they're all holed up in one room, perhaps waiting to be rescued,' replied Wilbur optimistically.

'Let's hope so.' Kennington started down the stairs. Suddenly his radio crackled and Henderson reported that all was well and that so far there was no sign of anyone and that he was going to continue the search on a lower level.

Gleeson stared around nervously, having now regretted venturing inside. A strong sense of claustrophobia bore down on him and it took a great mental effort not to scream out loud. Bile rose to his throat as a troubling thought developed in his brain — a thought that for the time being he forced himself to keep private, as it was so extreme and irrational that the very concept bordered on the insane.

Noting the professor's discomfort, Kennington turned to him. 'Maybe it would be best if you got out now. There's no telling what we mind find in the lower levels, and the last thing I need is for you to start playing up.'

'Don't worry about me. I'll be all right.'

'Suit yourself, but don't say I didn't warn you.' Kennington started down the stairs, the temperature dropping with each tread.

The level below was, like the one above, empty and predominately devoted to recreational spaces: a games room, a library, another mess room and a small gymnasium. However, everywhere they went they now found web-like patches of green slime adhering to the walls. Some of the furniture was likewise covered. In one room, a small cinema, a huge swath of web-slime stretched from the ceiling to the seats below.

The call came in from Henderson, reporting that he was now deep in the rig and that his party too had found great pools of slime. Some of the lower passages and rooms were impassable.

Kennington was about to call off when there was a dramatic change in Henderson's voice.

'Jesus Christ! What's that!?'

'Henderson?' Kennington shouted.

'Holy shit, you're not going to — '

The loud report of automatic gunfire blasted from the radio. Then came the screams. More gunfire was followed by a chittering, slurping noise and then silence.

★　★　★

An unsettling minute or so passed as the three men stared at each other in shock and horror. That something terrible had happened to the other team now seemed obvious, for there was no more radio contact.

'What do we do?' asked Gleeson, his face sickly-looking in the shadowy light.

'Time to go,' answered Kennington. 'We should never have come here in the first place.' He walked briskly for the exit and the passage leading back to the stairs.

They were crossing one of the rooms they had previously explored when something long, segmented and multi-legged detached itself from the ceiling and landed on Wilbur's head and shoulders. Like some snake-lobster hybrid, the thing's body coiled around the unfortunate marine's neck, as with a barbed stinger which dripped a green venom it stung him full in the chest, easily puncturing his protective suit.

'No!' Kennington yelled, his pistol raised, knowing that if he were to shoot he would in all probability hit Wilbur. Although, given the network of blue-violet veins that were breaking to the surface of his face and the manner in which his eyes bulged and reddened, maybe it would be for the best. With that thought, he pulled the trigger several times and turned to flee, only vaguely aware that Gleeson was already bounding up the stairs in front of him.

'Come on!' the professor shouted. 'Quick, get up here with the flashlight. I can't see a thing!'

Kennington leapt up the stairs. He shone his flashlight directly ahead. A short stretch of corridor was all that now separated them from escape.

Suddenly a door further along on the left burst open, and a dark wave of nauseating black liquid within which were contained shapes — human-like shapes, ghastly and screaming — poured forth. Squelching obscenely, the revolting oleaginous effluent crashed against the opposite wall, splashing halfway up to the ceiling before rushing forward towards the two men.

Gleeson was terror-stricken, paralysed with fear.

'*Run!*' Kennington gripped the professor and hauled him away, dragging him back the way they had come. With a powerful kick, he booted a door open, threw the other inside and slammed it shut behind him. His heart was thumping inside his chest, threatening to explode. Something was happening here that he could not even begin to understand. It seemed as though the thoughts that were moving and pulsing inside his brain were not his own, and he felt his sanity begin to slide away from him. Beyond the door, he could hear the slopping and squelching noises as that amorphous corpse-saturated stuff oozed outside. Then, to his horror, the metal door began to bulge inwards. Around the jambs and from underneath seeped pools of viscous blackness within which small, luminous, tadpole-like creatures swam and wriggled.

The two men backed away. With a loud crash, a door behind them was thrown open.

'*Colonel!*'

Kennington turned to see one of his marines — a young man named Steve Williams — standing in the doorway. His face was pale and bloodied, his protective suit covered in unsightly splatters of grey-green slime. Still, at least he was alive.

'Come on! There's another way back to the exit!' Williams shouted. 'Follow me!'

Tar-like midnight-black pseudopods bubbled into the room as Kennington and Gleeson dashed to join Williams. They had just reached the far door when the foul outpouring engulfed the metal portal and, like some hideous afterbirth, flooded into the room.

Chaos raged inside Kennington's normally highly disciplined mind as he ran, only dimly aware that Gleeson and Williams were ahead of him, their shadowy forms visible in the madly swinging flashlight. Then there came a burst of automatic gunfire as the young marine blasted something or other in his path. There was a high-pitched mewling sound, followed by the mass scuttling of dark shapes.

The passage they were charging along

seemed to be filled with small half-crab, half-trilobite-like creatures which scattered like a cascade of dropped marbles as they ran on, heading for the stairs at the far end. Gleeson screamed as one of the monstrosities fell from the ceiling, landed on his head and nipped at his face, seeking to gain purchase. It sheared off half of his right ear with one of its pincers. Yelling in agony, blood streaming down his face, he grabbed it and dashed it to the floor.

'Quick! Up the stairs!' Williams stood at an open door. Pushing the professor inside, he then gave a burst of covering fire which illuminated the dark passage, targeting whatever was on Kennington's heels. Slime sprayed.

Crunching some of the hideous creatures underfoot, Kennington sprinted for the door. Brushing past Williams, he started up the stairs.

The young marine stood his ground, putting down a deadly barrage of gunfire which rent the dark asunder, the deafening report mercifully drowning out much of the dreadful wails and cries that came from the darkness. After a few seconds of sustained shooting, he slammed the door shut and rushed up the stairs, joining the other two on a small landing from which two more doors gave access to other parts of the rig.

'You're the expert. What the hell's going on?' Kennington demanded, his eyes boring into Gleeson. 'And what are these *things*?'

The professor was wiping his glasses, his face streaked with sweat. 'I . . . I don't know. I honestly don't know. They're unlike anything I've ever seen before.'

'Thankfully, I don't think that blob-thing can get up the stairs,' said Williams.

Now that there was no imminent danger, Kennington asked, 'Henderson . . . and the others?' By way of answer, Williams shook his head. Kennington cursed volubly. There was an open door directly ahead of them which led to a long stretch of passageway. 'The canteen we first entered is at the end of this passageway,' he revealed. 'It looks clear.' Tentatively, he stepped out into the space beyond, his gun held out before him, ready and more than willing to blast anything that got in his way.

They were within ten yards of the canteen when a side door burst open and a grasping mass of black semi-solid tentacles shot forth. Through terror-stricken eyes, Kennington saw Williams engulfed as the multiple appendages lost much of their solidity and became more like an oleaginous flow which drenched the unfortunate marine from head to foot. Rapacious vine-like tendrils squirmed from the ceiling, grasping him around an upraised arm. The soldier screamed and tried to free himself even as the colonel and the professor backed away.

Somehow, Williams managed to pull himself upright, but in that next instant two more grasping pseudopods latched onto him — one coiling around his left leg, the other entwining itself about his right arm. Kicking and screaming, he was raised off the ground and held firm, like a fly trapped in a spider's web.

Thunder roared from within the canteen as two grenades dropped by those above exploded, peppering the room with deadly shrapnel and bringing down the ceiling directly ahead. A splatter of purplish goo gushed forward, burying Williams and blocking the way ahead.

★ ★ ★

Things other than flesh crawled down here. Things that scampered, scurried, slinked, skittered and slithered. Things that lacked name or identification. Things that no biologist, no matter how desperate for knowledge or fame, would care to study . . . at least not too closely.

For the time being, these horrors were absent, hanging back from Kennington's flashlight, their unnerving movements heard as opposed to seen, their very invisibility enough to instil terror into the two men. A demoralising fear-induced sickness had befallen them so that now, as they took refuge in a small storage area little larger than a closet, they dared not leave; and yet they knew that their survival necessitated them doing so. Unable to establish radio contact with the outside, and well aware that there was only so much battery life remaining in the flashlight, they knew they could not hide here indefinitely.

Thoughtfully, Kennington looked at his pistol, knowing full well that it would be of little use against the multitude of alien creatures that were out there, but —

'You might think me crazy, but I've had an idea going around my head regarding what's happening here.'

Kennington looked at Gleeson, the professor's words shaking him from his morbid thoughts. 'Go on.'

'These creatures — they're unlike any aquatic or terrestrial life forms known to man . . . and as for that disgusting jellied mass, well . . . ' Gleeson paused, unsure how to continue.

'Well what? Come on, spit it out!'

'Well . . . I think they're all acting as part of a whole. It's as though we're the intruder and they're the 'cleansing agent', for lack of a better description. The best explanation I can give is that these things are seeking to purge us from this rig. Like antibodies combating a disease within the human bloodstream. We're the infection

— don't you see?' There was a mad, staring look to Gleeson's face. He was shaking slightly, though whether due to the cold, fear or something else it was hard to tell. 'Yes, that's it!'

'You've lost me,' said Kennington.

'Imagine the rig's a mosquito. Its drill is the insect's proboscis, piercing deep into the earth, penetrating God alone knows what in an effort to extract a precious fluid. The casing which has formed around the drilling platform is the scab. These creatures are doing their best to eliminate us. It's as though we're the parasites!'

'Nonsense!' Kennington shook his head in disbelief, certain that the other had completely lost it. Christ, if that was the case, then just what the hell lay two miles or so beneath them? Some truly gargantuan, continent-sized, chthonic leviathan with an immune system comprised of nightmarish creatures? This theory was insane.

'We're never going to get out of here, and you know as well as I that they'll never send another rescue party,' Gleeson muttered.

'So, what do you suggest? Stay here until whatever's eradicated the others eradicates us?' replied Kennington. 'I say we wait for a while and then see about finding an alternative way to the canteen. There must be more than one route.'

'We'll die if we go out there.'

'Well I'd rather go down fighting than rot my life away hiding in here. Besides, think how it's going to be when the light gives up.'

Gleeson shivered at that very thought. It would be the most horrifying of experiences — sitting, huddled in the corner of this room, straining every sense in order to pick out the slow, insidious advancement of things eager for his blood.

★ ★ ★

Gun in one hand, flashlight in the other, Kennington edged his way forward, the professor close behind him. Each step was slow and silent. Navigating through this warren of corridors, stairways and rooms was tortuous and laden with terror, each new shadow or darkened opening a potential nightmare-in-waiting.

Both knew that death could come at any moment and from any direction. It was all around them; waiting, biding its time, readying itself for the strike. They were the flies blundering ever closer to the spider's web.

Kennington stopped. There was a sound, muffled and yet somehow familiar.

Gleeson heard it too. 'The helicopter! We must be near the canteen!' Emboldened by a new strength of purpose, he rushed for the nearest door and pushed it wide, finding with some relief that they had arrived at their access point. 'Help!' he shouted, hoping to alert those above.

Scanning the area and noting the damage wrought by the two hand grenades that had exploded earlier, Kennington stepped into the room. All was quiet. He paced over to the hole through which they had descended little over an hour ago — although it seemed a lot longer — and peered up, seeing nothing but the dark tube of strange jelly with a welcoming circle of blue sky beyond. His heart sank however as he heard the sounds of the helicopter diminishing.

'Help! For God's sake get us out of here!' Gleeson hollered up the pipe.

Gently chewing his bottom lip, Kennington tried to quickly think things through. It was clear that the remaining men had given up any hope of finding survivors, including the exploratory team, and had decided to head back. Perhaps they had been attacked by the same creature or creatures that had plagued him, hence the dropped grenades. In the end it came down to the same thing. They were now well and truly in the mire.

'They've . . . ' The professor stared at Kennington in utter bewilderment. 'They've . . . the bastards have left us here!'

'It would appear so.' With the use of one of the canteen tables, Kennington hoisted himself up to the ceiling. It was going to be hard work clambering back up the opening but he did not think it would prove impossible. Drawing his combat knife from its belt-sheath, he began to cut handholds into the walls of the spongy pipe. In this manner, he created a ladder of sorts and began to ascend.

'Go on! You can make it!'

His resolve strengthened by Gleeson's words of encouragement, Kennington climbed higher, forever fearful that he would lose his precarious grip and slip back down, crashing on the canteen table beneath him. This was far worse than the countless obstacle courses he had subjected his subordinates to — a vertical mud crawl. And then, just as he thought he was never going to make it, he reached the top. Digging his blade in deep, he pulled himself free and rolled over on to his back, feeling the warm, sane, welcoming sun on his face, physically and mentally exhausted. A sudden scream jolted him back into action.

'For God's sake, help me!'

Looking down, Kennington caught a fleeting glimpse of Gleeson before a tide of black liquid surged over him.

Vomiting a mouthful of bloated, maggot-like creatures, the unfortunate marine biologist broke to the surface, his face now covered in bleeding lesions. And then he was gone.

The sun was setting in a spectacular cauldron of crimson and yellow as it sank on the far horizon. A chill wind picked up as the temperature plummeted.

Kennington sat alone atop the vast, corrupted drilling platform gazing out across the expanse of sea, wondering about his chances of survival. It would be suicidal to jump into the sea, thirty miles or so from land; but he would consider it if anything were to emerge from the opening nearby. He could only cling to the possibility that morning would bring with it a surveillance craft of some kind. However, even these residual hopes were instantly shattered, as in the far distance he saw lights in the heavens, mere sparks that grew in intensity as they neared.

He began to pray as the first of the missiles zoomed unerringly towards him.

GRUB

Revenge is a dish best served . . .
wriggling.

'You say you're starving? Well, why don't you go ask that fella o'er there wi' the grey shirt if he's got owt? He looks the sort that might do pie an' chips an' mushy peas.'

'Away wi' you, lass. We're in Bangkok now, not Huddersfield. I can guarantee they'll not do mushy peas here.' Grumpy fifty-seven-year-old Yorkshireman Stan Brennan glowered at his wife before making his way through the bustling crowd and heading over to the street vendor.

Pleased to have attracted a prospective customer, the dishevelled man grinned, revealing his cracked and discoloured teeth. He picked up his small serving shovel and said in reasonably good English, 'Red ants — very nice and spicy.

135

Good for the digestion. Maybe you try worms in black bean sauce?' He lifted the wooden lid to one of his dishing-out pots in which an unsightly mass seethed and squirmed in a vile, oleaginous, slightly steaming soup. Something long and segmented slithered free and plopped to the litter-strewn pavement, whereupon it slinked into an open drain.

'Christ alive! What the hell have you got here?' Struck by a terrible stench, Brennan wafted aside the foul air in front of him. 'Are you sure it's all right to eat this stuff? I mean, no offence, but it looks horrible.' Mildly revolted, yet curious all the same, he stepped forward in order to examine some of the things on offer. There were battered maggots, deep-fried weevils, worms of different types, crispy-coated, kebabed scorpions, water beetles in various sauces and several other varieties of edible insect that he could not distinguish. Those that had not been cooked were still very much alive, skittering and wriggling in their serving trays.

'Yes, yes. Very nice.' The street vender nodded enthusiastically. 'Local delicacy.'

'Well, I've seen everything now.' Brennan turned to his wife. 'What say you, Mavis? Should I be brave an' try summat?'

Mavis frowned disapprovingly. It was hard enough looking at some of the food-stuffs on offer never mind eating them. 'It's enough to turn your stomach. Still, it's your innards.'

'Well, like they say, when in Thailand do as the Thais do. An' besides, 'don't knock it till you've tried it.' That's always been my motto.' Trying to keep his stomach in order, Brennan ran his gaze over the various unappetising things available. 'What would you recommend?'

'Try a mixed bag. I give you some water beetles, some weevils, some red ants and a few crickets,' replied the stall owner.

'That sounds . . . reasonable.'

The fast-food seller shovelled some of his wares into a paper bag. 'You want salt and vinegar?'

'Aye, go on then.'

'And as a little extra I give you some roach eggs.'

Brennan was not so sure about that. Ever since he had found a dead cockroach underneath his lettuce leaves one school dinner, he had had reason not to like them . . . or salad for that matter. 'Eh . . . maybe I'll skip the — '

'Very nice. Adds a distinctive flavour. Like ginseng, it give you extra staying power.' The street vendor gave a knowing wink.

'Oh, well, go on then. But don't overdo it.'

The insect-seller removed a packet from within the confines of his shirt, tore it open and sprinkled its contents in with the rest. He then gave the paper bag to his customer. 'Enjoy.'

Reaching into a trouser pocket, Brennan removed a few crumpled notes and handed them over. He looked warily for a moment at his 'snack'. Apart from the few crispy legs and the occasional protruding antennae, it *could* have been pork scratchings or chicken nuggets. That was what he would have to tell himself when it came to eating it.

'You want something else? Maybe something for the good lady? I do nice bamboo worm soup.'

Brennan turned to his wife. 'I take it

you're not on for some, are you, luv?'

Mavis shook her head, her lined face pale and sickly-looking.

'Are you all right?' Brennan asked.

'I think I'm going to be — ' Mavis' cheeks swelled and it appeared as though she was about to vomit.

'Bloody hell, woman! It's just deep-fried bugs.' Fighting back his own sense of revulsion, Brennan picked out a bite-sized morsel, examined it briefly and then put it into his mouth. For a sickening moment he had a mental image of the nugget sprouting legs and skittering around his mouth before vanishing down his throat. He gagged for a second and then bit into it, feeling the gooey, wet squirt as his dentures broke through the layers of crispy fat and chitin, rupturing the soft, gelatinous inner body. It was only partially cooked. Still, he began chewing. Now that the initial shock was fading, he found himself rather enjoying the taste — peanutty, with a hint of . . . marzipan. It gave a completely new meaning to the term *grub* all the same.

Her immediate bout of nausea over,

Mavis regained her composure and the two of them made their way through the bustling, noisy market.

Vendors called out, seeking customers for their myriad wares. Everywhere people jostled and clamoured. Horns blared as battered cars and folk on mopeds navigated the busy dust-filled roads, filling the air with the reek of exhaust fumes. Sleazy-looking men and scantily clad women hung around the entrances to some of the decrepit buildings.

'It reminds me o' Grimsby,' commented Brennan jocularly. He began munching through his takeaway as though it was nothing more unusual than a bag of chips.

'Well? What's it like?' Mavis asked after a few minutes. She was disgusted, yet curious all the same.

'It's rather nice.' Brennan helped himself to some more, his fingers becoming greasy. It was different, there was no denying that, but it was not altogether unpleasant. Quite the opposite in fact. Now that his taste buds had become accustomed to the unusual sensation and texture, it was proving to be quite the culinary experience.

'Sure you don't want to try a bit?' He held out a piece that was pink on the inside, like Turkish delight.

Mavis shook her head emphatically. 'You bet I'm sure. If you want to play Russian roulette with your innards, that's up to you, but don't come crying to me if you end up throwing your guts down the bog.'

'You know you really should try some. Surely you'd agree it'd be a shame to visit Thailand and eat nowt but McDonalds an' cheese an' pickle sarnies. You've got to be a bit more adventurous, Mavis. Why, each country has its own speciality which we'd consider odd. France has its snails and frogs' legs. Japan has a highly poisonous pufferfish. Peru has roast guinea pigs . . . and if you knew what the old Jocks put in haggis, odds are you'd never go to a Burns Night Supper again.'

★ ★ ★

'It's *Phoo-ket*,' Alan Thompson corrected after the laughter resulting from the waspish Yorkshire woman's mispronunciation had died down. He was a youthful forty-something-year old with tanned features and dyed blond hair, dressed in a pair of Bermuda shorts and a Hawaiian shirt.

'Oh?' Mavis muttered, an embarrassed look on her face. She was sat with three others, having her evening meal in the hotel. She looked again towards the toilets. This was the fourth time her husband had been forced to make a dash for it.

'Yes, I ditched the wife, said goodbye to the kids and the nine-to-five job that was driving me round the bend, and started a small diving school out here a few years ago,' Thompson went on. 'Best thing I ever did. Things have been on the up ever since. We get a lot of Europeans and Americans over in Phuket. The marine life is spectacular and the waters are so clear it's ideal for snorkelling. You really should come and visit.'

Mavis merely nodded.

'Is your husband all right?' asked the young man on her left. He had introduced himself as Mark Smith and he was on honeymoon with his wife, Samantha — a dark-haired, pretty woman who had said little all evening. From their dress and mannerisms, it was obvious that both were cultured, well-educated, and from the sounds of it rather wealthy. They came from Kent.

'I think it's just the heat an' the foreign food. You know what it's like,' Mavis answered. She nibbled at a prawn cracker.

'This is your first night, is it not?' Thompson asked.

Mavis nodded. 'We arrived early this morning. We've never been abroad before.'

'I thought as much.' Thompson took a sip from his wine glass. 'It takes several days to adjust to Thailand; both the climate and, most importantly, the food. My advice would be to stick to the plainer stuff. Food that you're used to. At least for the first week or so. Then, when you've built up a level of immunity, become a bit more adventurous. Trust me, I've seen many people come here thinking that they can stomach some of the local specialities. Most do so out of bravado, believing it makes them look tough in the eyes of their friends or it will sound good when they get back home.

Unfortunately, most of them end up spending three or four days in bed.'

'Stan did go for a bag o' mixed insects, even though I told him not to,' Mavis admitted.

'Insects aren't usually so bad,' said Thompson. 'In fact, they're one of the safer options here in Thailand. Worms, maggots, ants, weevils . . . they're all highly nutritious and packed with protein. I'd be a little wary about going for scorpions or spiders, however, as — '

'Please . . . we're trying to eat here,' complained Smith. Like his taciturn wife, he had gone for the safer option of steak and chips from the 'British menu'.

'I do apologise. So, what brings you out to Thailand?' Thompson asked, his question levelled at the young couple.

'I was born here,' Smith revealed. 'My parents worked in the diplomatic service in Bangkok. So it seemed a natural choice for our honeymoon.'

'And you?' Thompson asked Mavis.

'Well . . . my husband had a little win on the lottery a couple o' months back. So we thought we'd treat ourselves.'

Mavis deliberately held back saying anything about Stan wanting to come out here to prospect for younger women.

'What is it you both do?' Thompson asked conversationally.

'I used to be a lollipop woman at the nearby school, an' my husband works, or rather worked, for the Gas Board.' Mavis was about to say something more when she saw Stan exit the toilets. There was a drawn look to his face.

'Christ! I needed that,' announced Brennan, taking his seat next to his wife. Not one for social etiquette, he went straight into a detailed account of his time sat on the toilet, which prompted Mr. and Mrs. Smith to hurriedly finish their meal and leave, making an excuse that they had an early excursion to visit some nearby ruins in the morning.

Thompson was not so easily put off. 'Are you sure you're feeling okay?' he asked.

'Aye . . . I am that. Better out than in, as they say.' Brennan heaped some rice and noodles on to his fork and shovelled it into his mouth. 'Say, you must know the local area. Where should we go if we're looking for a little nightlife?'

'There are bars all over town. Most stay open all night. Tell you what, Mr. Brennan. I'll get you a drink and write down the addresses of a few places I know.'

'Only the one drink,' Mavis cautioned. She turned to her husband. 'At any rate, I doubt whether we'll be going anywhere tonight. It'll be your bed after you've had your meal.'

★ ★ ★

Mavis' prediction had proved to be right. For it was now after midnight, and for the past hour and a half Brennan had been sat on the toilet, the excruciating cramps in his stomach sometimes so severe they made him wail with agony.

'Stop whining, will you?' said Mavis unsympathetically from where she stood in the doorway. 'You're nowt but a big blubbering baby. Just think what the Braithwaites from Number Twenty-Two would say if they could see you now.'

'I couldn't give a monkey's! Aaaaggh!

Jesus!' Brennan sat, slumped, one hand gripping the edge of the sink, the other, palm outward, against the tiled wall. He cursed volubly and continued to moan.

'It's your own stupid fault for eating all those bloody beetles an' things. Christ knows what that's done to your insides.'

'Just shut up, will you?' Brennan groaned.

'You're the one who's making all the noise. At this rate you'll end up waking everybody else in the hotel and then we'll probably get flung out.'

Brennan moaned again, louder this time. The pain in his guts was dreadful. It was how he imagined being disembowelled would feel. His stomach began gurgling like an overfilled sewage pipe.

'Why the hell did we decide to come here in the first place? I knew we should o' just gone to Scarborough like we normally do.' Coming to the realisation that she was not going to get much sleep with how things currently were, Mavis lit a cigarette. She took a deep drag. 'You get proper food there. Fish an' chips. Black pudding. None o' this foreign muck. We could've gone an' stayed wi' my mother.'

The obscene rumblings from inside Brennan were becoming louder and more unpleasant-sounding. There was a bad stink coming from him.

Mavis continued talking, oblivious to her suffering husband, her words becoming louder. 'But no! You wanted to come here. Bangkok. Why, even the name sounds a bit rude and as for that other place I bet that's not called *Phoo-ket* wi'out good reason. Well, don't think you've pulled wool o'er my eyes, Stan Brennan! I know you only wanted to come out here so as you could see what the women were like. Aye, I bet you've read summat in the paper or heard from one o' your pals down the Dog an' Duck about all those young Thai brides looking for men so as they can come an' live in England. Well, I think it's disgusting! That's what it is, plain an' — '

With a tremendous fart, Brennan was lifted clear off the toilet seat. He flew for several feet and collided, head-first, with the wall. Knocked back, he fell, cracked his head off the porcelain sink and crumpled to the bathroom floor.

In the darkness, Stan could hear voices. They were whispering, conspiratorial voices that seemed to spiral through the dark depths of his confused brain as though they were mere memories; fragments of speech from another time and place. The first that registered was that of a man. The other belonged to a woman and sounded very familiar.

'You've played a blinder, Mavis. Now, are you sure he's dead?'

'Aye. He must be. He hasn't moved for the past hour or so. He's still lying flat out in the bathroom.'

'Good.'

'So what do we do now?'

'Listen carefully. I want you to phone the emergency services. Tell them that your husband's suffered a heart attack. Tell them where he can be found. Then, when they arrive, make your way over to my place just behind where my food stall was and we'll go from there. Don't worry, it'll be pretty obvious to the ambulance crew that he's died of natural causes, so there won't be an immediate police investigation.'

'You're absolutely sure they won't do blood tests and discover the drug in his system?'

'They might do tests, but rest assured they won't find anything. Now, I'd better get back so as I can make the necessary preparations. I'll see you in about an hour.'

The voices in Stan's head ceased.

Some time later he sensed movement. The rumble of tyres. He opened his eyes and a harsh, white light stabbed down at him.

The paramedic screeched in shock and sprang back from the gurney to which the fat English tourist had been strapped. Having found no vital signs at the scene, he had been sure that the man was dead, and had only chosen to ride in the back of the ambulance to fill in the paperwork. Trying to recover his professional demeanour, he started to check his patient over. 'Please lie still, sir. You're going to hospital.'

'O'er my dead body!' Brennan exclaimed. 'Can't stand the places. Hospitals are where sick folk go to die.' He sat up, seemingly oblivious to the tearing sound of the restraining straps breaking. 'There's nowt wrong wi' me. I just had a nasty turn back there.' He paused, remembering the voices he had heard after he had blacked out. He realised that the woman had been his wife, as unsympathetic as ever, but the man's voice was troubling him more. It seemed to remind him of someone. Struggling to replay the overheard conversation, he gasped as it came to him. It had been that poncey diver bloke they had met at dinner. Another memory was prodding its way through his marshmallow brain — an image of his wife back at home, typing or texting or whatever the hell she did on that bloody Facebook. She spent more time corresponding with folk she knew through the internet than she ever did with him.

Desperately, the paramedic tried to get his miraculously recovered patient to lie down.

The image of Thompson's tanned grinning face hung before Brennan. Dye his hair black and give him a moustache and it was the same man he had seen in passing many times at home on his wife's recently purchased computer — a little gift he had bought her after the six-ball lottery win had made him a millionaire several times over. And now that smarmy git was here in Thailand, conspiring with Mavis, making out that he was a diving instructor. The Yorkshireman swore as he realised that Thompson had also disguised himself as the dodgy street vendor. It was all coming clear to him. How long had this 'relationship' been going on for? How long had this all been planned? Despite his wife's claims to the contrary, it had been she who had suggested visiting Thailand, not him. The conniving bastards had tried to poison him in order to get their grubby hands on his newly won fortune! It was not he who had come to Thailand to find a younger wife but rather she who had come out here to find a younger husband. He would bet all the money he had that Thompson was not interested in her charm or her looks — not that she had either — but only in the money she was set to inherit.

'Sir! You must calm down,' the

paramedic was pleading. 'You've had a heart attack.'

Brennan cursed. His vision was blurry. He wanted to get out of the ambulance. He turned to the frightened Thai. 'Heart attack?'

'Yes, that's what your wife said.'

'Rubbish. There's nowt wrong wi' my heart. I'm as fit as a fiddle.'

'But . . . you were dead!'

'Dead, my arse!' Brennan said. 'Now, let me out of here!'

The paramedic tried rather feebly to argue with his patient but in truth he wanted nothing more than to be rid of the crazy man. He thumped on the partition between him and the driver, shouting loudly in Thai. The driver stopped the ambulance to see what was going on for himself.

As soon as the vehicle had come to a halt, Brennan wrenched open the doors and jumped from the ambulance. He began sniffing the air. He then let out a hiss of satisfaction and strode off, clad only in a white sheet which he had pulled tight around his body. Alarmingly, he noticed that his chest and abdomen had become a rippling surface of pale, flabby flesh. He felt his throat swell, and then from out of his open mouth scurried a large black cockroach. Then came another. And another. They fell to the ground and began scurrying around his bare feet.

A bus went past, throwing up a cloud of noisome exhaust fumes.

Unable to scream, Brennan watched in horror as an unsightly flood of skittering night-black cockroaches now poured from his mouth. He felt a pressure in his brain and then he was aware of his right eye popping out as an antennae-like protuberance emerged from the bloody orifice. There was a loud tearing sound in his head. Moments later, he saw a black, chitinous appendage burst from just below his ribcage. A searing pain lanced through him as he fell to his knees; a second, serrated, insectoid limb rupturing through his skin. Crawling to a darkened alley, his strangely heightened senses became aware of the multitude of beings around him, for, despite the early morning hour, the streets of downtown Bangkok were still busy.

Skulking through the labyrinth of streets, Brennan crept his way back to the vicinity of his hotel. Whereas most people, having experienced such a radical metamorphosis to both the mind and the body, would have quite probably succumbed to full-blown insanity, his mind was deeply rooted on one thing alone — vengeance. Mavis and her 'lover-boy' had assumed him dead. Well they were in for one hell of a rude awakening.

Up ahead, through eyes that, as far as he was concerned, had become bug-like; compound, multi-faceted, black orbs through which things registered in a science fiction B-movie kind of way, he could distinguish the stall where he had got his dodgy insect takeaway, behind which was a ramshackle shop.

Brennan grinned maniacally upon noticing that a back door was open. That would be Mavis's fault, he reasoned, knowing full well that she never could remember to lock their door at home. He staggered forward, unbalanced by the heavy carapace he could feel on his back. Looking around, he saw a row of windows and walked over to peer in. There was plenty of light from the street lamps and he caught sight of his own reflection. To his surprise, he saw a red-faced half-naked man wearing nothing but a torn sheet. No mandibles, no antennae, no exoskeleton. He flexed his pincers and the reflection clenched its fists, but then the image changed again and he saw his sleek, black insectoid body once more. Dismissing the anomaly from his mind, he concentrated on exacting his revenge. Looking directly through the window, he could make out what appeared to be a workshop. To his right, there were a couple of large barrels and a makeshift kitchen area with a few camping gas stoves on a long table. There were also several large vats and a collection of glass tubes and flasks. This had to be where Thompson concocted his insect food, poisonous or otherwise.

Striding to the door, Brennan paused for a moment then stepped inside. There was a sudden cry of surprise from the back of the room where Thompson and Mavis were seated at a table, celebrating with a bottle of champagne and planning how to spend the millions she was set to inherit. Now they stared in shock at the wild-eyed figure clad only in a sheet before them.

Mavis dropped her glass and screamed. 'It's Stan's ghost!'

Thompson swore and picked up the bottle. 'That's no ghost! The dose can't have been strong enough. Looks like I'll have to finish the job myself.'

Brennan bellowed his rage and leapt at Thompson, ducking under the man's wild swing and grabbing him round the waist. The Saturday mornings he had spent playing rugby as a boy came back to him and he threw all his considerable weight into the move, knocking the air from the younger man's lungs. Futilely, he tried to slice into the other's face with his mandibles but found they were having no effect.

'Get off me, you crazy bastard!' Thompson yelled. 'Hell, he's trying to bite me!' He managed to get his arm free and savagely brought the nearly empty bottle crashing down on his attacker's head.

Glass shattered and Stan staggered back. He recovered quickly, however; and, hissing his wrath, he launched himself at Thompson once more. Grabbing an outstretched arm and utilising his weight advantage, he spun his foe around and swung him face first into a wall.

Thompson cried out as he and the brickwork collided. Dazed, he staggered back several steps and then crumpled to the floor.

Despite his bulk and his drug-induced state, Brennan was quick. He dashed over to Thompson and, hauling him by his hair, frogmarched him towards one of the large vats. He had guessed correctly that there would be a hideous insect broth inside, and the smell which sweated from its now cooling stock was dreadful.

'No!' Thompson yelled.

With a cry of rage, Brennan plunged his would-be poisoner's face into the open-mouthed container. Dark-shelled things rose to the surface as he thrust

Thompson's head in deeper.

'Let him go!' cried Mavis.

Maintaining his pressure on Thompson's head, the half-man, half-bug-thing that Brennan now fervently believed he had become turned and focused its pitiless compound eyes on his scheming, murderous wife. His mouth widened and he chattered his teeth before forcibly hauling his victim free. Turning, he gazed into the drenched face, noticing that several creepy crawlies had now latched themselves on to his flesh whilst others were glued to the unfortunate's hair. 'You like diving. Let's see how long you can hold your breath!' Unmercifully, he dunked his victim a second time.

The insect-laden soup bubbled as Thompson frantically sought to break free.

Out of the corner of his eye — or rather the prismed multi-perspective sight that his brain now registered — Brennan caught sight of a bag of white crystals not dissimilar to the 'roach eggs' that had been added to his takeaway the day before. He reached out and upended the entire bag into the vat. Some of it landed in Thompson's hair but most of it fell into the foul soup.

The liquid in the vat frothed as its constituency altered, becoming thicker, sludgier.

After the best part of a minute, Brennan dragged his victim free and threw him to one side.

Gasping for breath, Thompson reeled before falling to his knees. His hands clasped around his throat as he tried to vomit. Gargling like a cat with a fur ball, he dry-retched several times before curling up into a foetal position. Wracked with pain, he began to convulse, his limbs and body jerking spasmodically.

Satisfied with his actions, Brennan stepped away.

Mavis rushed over and tried to help Thompson who was being violently sick on the floor.

Thompson's face and shirt were a mess and his pupils were heavily dilated. He began frothing at the mouth. Blood streamed from the corners of his eyes and from his nostrils.

'He's dying,' Mavis sobbed hysterically

'Probably not,' Brennan replied, examining the convulsing man with interest. 'He's just getting a taste of his own medicine. You know, the stuff you tried to kill me with.' Now that he had the upper hand he felt calmer and it seemed that the mind-warping effects of the poison were gradually lessening. The arthropod legs had vanished, although there remained a ghostly trace akin to the 'phantom limb' sensation often experienced by amputees. The kaleidoscopic images he had been seeing were settling back into normal vision.

Thompson had stopped writhing and now lay still.

'Alan!' Mavis screamed. She shook him but there was no response. 'You've killed him!' She turned on Brennan and began hitting him madly but without much effect. 'You've ruined everything!'

'For Christ's sake, woman! You were quite happy to do away wi' me. If he's dead, which I doubt, it would serve him right!' He took hold of Mavis's arms and pushed her away. 'Why did you do it anyway? I thought we were all right together.'

Mavis stared at him with fury. 'Because you're so bloody boring, Stan Brennan. I could stand it when we were poor. All the scrimping and saving. All the times you said: 'Oh no, we don't want to go abroad. It's not for us, we wouldn't like it'. Well, *I* would've liked it! And then, when you won enough money to really *live*, you put it into the building society, and we only moved round the corner to bloody Charlton Street.' She sneered at him. 'You've no ambition, no sense of adventure. When I found Alan, he said that it was a waste you having all that money and I have to agree. We planned a million and one things to do with it.'

'If you were that unhappy, you could've asked for a divorce! You didn't have to kill me!'

'Alan said — '

'I don't give a damn about 'Toy Boy' Thompson and his ideas. Anyway, look where they got him. Face down in a vat of slime. Bloody hell woman, are you daft? Can't you see he was just after your money, or rather *my* money?' Brennan looked down at Thompson and saw that the man was beginning to stir. 'Looks like he's not dead, though,' he added with slight disappointment.

Thompson made a strange gurgling sound and got slowly to his hands and knees. He shook his head irritably as if something was stuck in his ears.

'Alan, darling. Are you all right?' Mavis gasped crouching down beside him.

Thompson gave no sign that he had heard her, he just crawled unsteadily forward. His face was chalk-white. Ugly things crawled in his bleached hair.

'Alan!' Mavis repeated. 'Should I get you to a doctor?'

Thompson scurried to a shadowy corner of the room, ignoring her completely.

'What's wrong wi' you?' Mavis wailed, getting to her feet.

Brennan began to laugh as he finally realised what was going on. 'He thinks he's a bug! That 'roach egg' concoction he cooked up — it's hallucinogenic, not lethal.' He ran his hands over his head, checking for antennae, but there was nothing there except his own thinning hair. 'It made me believe I was turning into an insect.' He walked over to the windows and peered at his own blessedly normal reflection.

'You shut up Stan! You should've been dead by now.' Mavis turned on her husband, the vivid hatred and disgust twisting her features. 'Look what you've done to him!' She gestured to Thompson but then let out a cry.

The curled up shape was beginning to change. Thompson's soaked shirt was splitting as a hard black shell emerged from the torn fabric and his face was becoming more angular by the second.

Mavis screamed again and started to back away from the mutating man.

The massive dose of doctored 'roach eggs' had caused more than hallucinations this time.

Brennan felt his stomach turn over as he watched the transformation work its way through Thompson's body, taking over the human flesh, morphing him into a giant cockroach.

With a final shudder, Thompson's last shreds of humanity vanished and the new creation made a chittering sound as it hungrily surveyed the two before it . . .

DEAD ON ARRIVAL?

*A night in the morgue just got a
lot livelier...*

There was something very puzzling about
this whole affair, thought Doctor Nathan
Webb to himself as he sat in the small
office annexed to the hospital morgue and
read through the notes on the two corpses
— a man and a woman — that had been
delivered a couple of hours ago. Through
the glass window, he could see the covered lifeless forms lying on the operating
tables in the adjacent room. Neither had
as yet been formally identified, something
which the police were currently trying to
rectify. However, the cause of death was
as grotesque as it was mystifying, and he
would love to know the circumstances
behind the discovery.

The dead man was in his mid-thirties
and perfectly average from a morphologi-
cal point of view with no discerning

marks, scars or tattoos. Something — probably some kind of wild animal, perhaps a large canine — had torn his throat out. There was even a large bite, inflicted by undoubtedly the same fanged creature, on his right arm; where, it was reasoned, he had tried to protect himself.

However, the woman . . .

Webb read through the medical notes again — notes which had been written in Doctor Chris Laidler's spidery handwriting. Had they been produced by anyone but Laidler, his highly respected superior at the hospital, he would have been compelled to check the findings himself.

The woman, brown-skinned and perhaps of Thai or Malayan origin, had been decapitated in the most brutal fashion. The brief forensic tests that Laidler had performed prior to reaching the decision to continue his investigations in the morning, revealed that most of her internal organs were also missing, along with her head; her chest and abdominal areas now empty cavities. It was, as he wrote in his report: ' . . . as though her head has been torn off with such violence that her insides have been withdrawn as well.'

Webb shook his head in disbelief. He had spent ten years working down here, in a part of the hospital commonly referred to as 'Frankenstein's Laboratory', and had never known anything like it.

To the best of his knowledge, the police were 'keeping an open mind' as to the cause of death, but he had little doubt that they were linked. It was all so strange. Bizarre and unsettling. Still, it was not for him to speculate what could possibly have transpired. All he had to do was sit his shift out and wait until Laidler arrived in the morning.

Unbeknownst to him, they were going to be the most nightmarish few hours of his life.

★ ★ ★

Webb was going through the medical notes on some of the other cadavers they had in cold storage when the phone rang. Recognising the caller's number on the screen, he picked up the receiver and, doing his best Vincent Price impersonation, said: 'Frankenstein's Laboratory. Igor speaking. The master's out at the moment. Is there anything I can do for you?'

'For Christ's sake, Webb. How many times have I told you to stop doing that? It might have been funny the first time but it ain't anymore.'

'Lighten up, Charlie. Just having a bit of fun with you. Hell, you need to have a bit of a laugh now and then down here or else you'd go nuts. Anyway, what do you want?'

'There's a cop from the NYPD at reception looking for you. Well, when I say looking for you, I think he wants to talk with whichever doc's working the graveyard shift in the morgue. He says that he was here earlier with old Laidler. His name's White. Detective Bill White.'

'Oh yeah. I met him just as he was leaving. Did he say what he wants?'

'Not to me. Should I send him down?'

'Yes, I suppose you'd better.'

'Okay.'

Webb put the phone down and went to the entrance of the morgue, wincing slightly as a sudden vinegary tang, distinguishable from the numerous other chemical smells, struck his nostrils. The morgue was at one end of a long striplight-lit corridor from which many other doors gave access to other rooms and passageways. Halfway along were the stairs which led up to the ground floor, and he waited in silence for the echoing footsteps which would herald the arrival of his visitor. He did not have to wait long before Detective White appeared on the scene — a short, stocky man dressed in a damp black raincoat.

White raised a hand when he caught sight of the doctor. He began marching down the corridor.

'Detective. Nice to see you again,' greeted Webb. 'I see you don't get much sleep either.'

'It's all part of the job,' replied White. 'Do you mind if we have a talk? There's some things that just aren't adding up and I can't afford to wait till morning.'

'By all means. Come on in.' Webb held the door open, permitting White to enter.

He ushered the other towards the office, noting the strange manner in which the detective glanced at the two recently brought in corpses. One could have been forgiven for thinking that he was scared of something.

White took a seat.

'Would you like a coffee?' Webb asked from where he stood by the small vending machine. 'I go through half a dozen cups — '

'Has anything strange happened?' White interrupted. 'Anything . . . out of the ordinary?'

For a moment Webb was at a loss for words, uncertain how to respond. He took his seat opposite the detective. 'Strange? What do you mean?'

White scratched his head. 'I dunno. Anything . . . *weird*?' He looked over his shoulder, through the glass window into the operating theatre.

Webb could clearly see the man's reflection in the glass, and it was the face of a man in fear. It was almost as though he was half-expecting to see something ghastly emerge from the shadows or for the cadaver-lockers to slide open debouching their zombie contents. The doctor shook his head. 'Nothing unusual. Why do you ask? Are you expecting something? Something I should know about?' He asked this last question with some measure of concern, suddenly reminded of the time when a psychopathic, violent drug dealer had caused mayhem searching for a body in which were stashed bags of dope. He had not been on duty that night, but one of his colleagues had spent days in one of the wards upstairs after having been badly beaten.

White turned round. 'You've probably guessed it's to do with those two stiffs that were brought in earlier. The two you've got lying out there.'

'The man and the woman?'

'Yes. Mr. Henry North and . . . Miss Boon-Mee.' White struggled to get the woman's name out.

'So you've managed to identify them?'

'Yes.' White reached into a pocket of his coat and removed a small black book. 'This was found in Mr. North's jacket pocket. Now . . . I can't with any honesty say that I'm a religious man, nor do I believe in the supernatural; however, I've spent the last hour or so going through this, which to be honest with you proves extremely hard reading.'

'You've got me interested. What is it?'

'First, may I ask if you're aware of the Staten Island child abductions?'

'Of course. It's been on the news and in the papers for months. How many kids have gone missing so far? Ten? Eleven?'

'Eleven,' White answered sharply.

'Why do you ask?'

'Well, it's just possible that the culprit's lying in the room next door.'

'Jesus!' Webb's mouth hung slackly open.

'Is it me or is it hot in here?' Loosening his tie, the detective then dabbed at his forehead with his fingertips, wiping away a sheen of sweat.

'It's not cold, that's for sure.'

White shifted in his seat.

'When you say the culprit, I take it you mean the man — this Mr. North?' Webb's eyes were drawn to the black book.

'No. I mean *her*.'

'Miss Boon-May?'

'Boon-Mee,' White corrected. He turned round in order to look into the morgue once more. 'Although I doubt if that's her real name. I doubt if — ' He gave a sudden startled cry and sprang out of his chair, his hand going for his gun.

Webb got out of his seat. 'Detective?'

'The . . . sheet. Did you see it? Did you see it move?'

'What are you talking about?' Webb went to the office door and pushed it open. The operating chamber where he and Doctor Laidler had performed hundreds of autopsies was bathed in a sharp actinic light which did little to make the morgue look welcoming.

White held his revolver in a shaking hand. He pointed towards the closest sheet-covered body, that of the decapitated Oriental woman. 'It moved.'

'Eh?' Webb was unsettled. Had this been Halloween, and had this been one of his colleagues telling him this, he might have put it down as a sick joke; but an NYPD detective making such an observation bordered on the downright macabre.

'I saw it. I saw the sheet move.'

'You're kidding me, right?'

'I'm telling you. I saw it move.'

A sickly knot of fear was tightening in Webb's stomach, and he could almost hear his heart thudding against his ribs. His mind screamed at him and he found himself gulping nervously. Death was his business — the examination of the dead something he had lived with for over ten years; but never had he been faced with anything like this. In his well-ordered sane world, the dead stayed dead; and even though he had read of one or two very rare cases when someone mistakenly pronounced dead had been brought in with the DOA toe tags, this woman's head and guts were missing. There could be no mistake. Horrible thoughts boiled within his brain, conjuring terrible images which were no doubt given substance by the countless horror films he had watched over the years. Was it just his imagination, or did the sheet twitch a little? It was impossible, he tried to tell himself.

White was backing away towards the door. It was obvious that he was ready to make a dash for it if anything out of the ordinary were to happen.

This was crazy, Webb told himself. Absolute madness. Managing to put things back into perspective, he dismissed his earlier notion that the cover had moved. Pacing over to the corpse, he dragged the sheet clear.

Boon-Mee's headless remains were motionless; seventy or so pounds of dead, naked flesh — gutted like an animal. That unpleasant vinegary stink was stronger and seemed to be coming from the corpse itself.

Webb did the respectful thing and covered her up again. He turned to the detective. 'She's still dead. I guess you must have imagined seeing the cover move. Believe me, I've spent many a time down here on my own and I'll be the first to admit it can get a little creepy. The mind can play havoc if you let it.'

'Are you sure . . . she's dead?'

'Absolutely.' The very fact that she was headless was surely evidence of that.

Slowly, White edged his way back from the exit.

'Do you think we can go back to the

office so that you can tell me more about what's going on?' asked Webb. His own thoughts were gradually returning to normal, although he would be the first to admit that he had, for a minute or so, been more than a little frightened.

'Okay.' White's eyes were constantly on the covered cadaver as he made his way back into the small room. He took his seat.

'Are you all right?' The doctor asked concernedly as he too returned to his chair.

White smiled and nodded unconvincingly.

'I believe Doctor Laidler keeps a small bottle of the hard stuff lying around somewhere if you're in need of a drink.'

White waved a hand. 'No. That won't be necessary.' He reached out for the book which still lay on the table before him. 'From what I can gather, this was written by Henry North, who was the father of one of the missing youngsters. The first dozen or so pages are concerned mainly with his own investigations into the disappearances; and from a cursory skim through, it's pretty obvious that he didn't think much of how the police were handling things. Anyway, he mentions covering all the areas where the kids vanished, conducting door-to-door inquiries, talking to several of the other parents and so on. However, it's in the second half of the book that things — '

The phone rang, causing Webb to jump. He did not recognise the caller's number. He picked up the receiver. 'Doctor Webb. St Michael's Hospital.'

'Is . . . is she still . . . '

It was a woman's voice, but the words were heavily accented. Maybe Spanish, thought Webb. The line was not too good either. 'Sorry, I can't — '

'Is she still there?'

'Is she still there?' Webb repeated, unsure if he had heard correctly. Calling a morgue at half-past one in the morning to ask if someone was still there was one hell of a prank to play. It was not as though those in his care were likely to go anywhere. With that thought, a tingle of ice crept along his spine. 'Who? Who do you want to speak to? This is Doctor Nathan Webb.'

'Is she still there?' The voice was stronger now, demanding.

'Look, I don't know what you're talking about. I think you've got the wrong number.' Webb put the phone down.

'Who was it?' asked White.

Webb shook his head. 'I've no idea.'

The phone went again. Webb picked it up, somewhat relieved to see it was the number for Charlie at the main reception.

'Doctor Webb?'

'Charlie?'

'I take it you got your call?'

'Yes. Any idea who it was? Did she leave a contact number?'

'No, a foreign-sounding woman phoned about ten minutes ago asking for your private number. I take it that was her. I tried to tell her that she should wait until morning, but she was very persistent. She said it was a matter of life and death. Something about a friend of hers having been in a terrible accident. She'd been informed that she'd been brought here.'

'I see.' Webb felt a pang of guilt. 'Well, put her straight through if she calls again.'

'Will do.'

Webb put the phone down. 'The mysterious caller claims to be a friend of the deceased woman.' He looked at White questioningly. 'I notice from the notes that there's no information whatsoever regarding how the injuries were sustained, estimated time or indeed location, which I find highly unusual. Perhaps you can fill me in.'

'One of my officers was alerted to what at first was assumed to be a break-in at an abandoned property off Fedderson Avenue in the Bronx. A passing member of the public reported hearing 'unearthly' screams and shouts coming from one of the upstairs windows. Inside, the officer came across a scene of absolute carnage. North and Boon-Mee were found in the hall and . . . and several other bodies, mostly children, I'm afraid to say, were found in the basement.'

'Bloody hell!'

'The dead kids have been sent to Saint Vincent's, but it appears as though they've all been drained of blood.'

'Christ! There's some sick bastards out there.'

'Anyway, back to the book for this is

where the really interesting clues lie.' White flicked through several pages. 'As I said, I've only skimmed through it, but either it's the ramblings of a madman — a man perhaps driven mad with grief over his lost daughter and the obsessional search he undertook to try and find her — or . . . well, I'll let you decide.'

'Before you go any further, I've a question for you, Detective.' Webb leaned forward, resting his elbows on the desk and interlacing his fingers. 'If I get you right, your theory as it stands runs something like this: For reasons that have still to be established, Mr. North, believing he had found the whereabouts of the child murderer, stole into Boon-Mee's house in order to confront her? Yes?'

White nodded.

'Yet, that doesn't explain the nature of the injuries. This man's been savaged by a ferocious creature, and if he murdered Boon-Mee, why — and more to the point *how* — did he do it in such a barbaric way? There's a lot here that just doesn't make sense.'

'This is where the book comes in. But

you're not going to believe what I'm about to tell you. Hell, I don't know whether I believe it, however it's apparent that Mr. North did. To the extent that it cost him his life.'

'Well, what is it?'

White flicked through several pages. 'Here. This is it.' He handed the book over.

There was a crude drawing of a long-haired woman's head, her eyes mad and staring, her mouth wide open and fang-filled. From the severed neck dangled an unsightly mass of tangled insides complete with lungs, heart, stomach and intestines. It was incredibly repulsive, yet as a medical professional, Webb had to acknowledge its anatomical detail.

'North refers to it as a penanggalan,' said White, seeing the confusion on the doctor's face. He read directly from the book: 'A southeast Asian female vampire-like creature which feeds on the blood of the young. By day it appears as a normal woman, attractive, the kind of person you could easily pass in the street; but by night, and when on the hunt, it transforms into a most horrible entity. The head detaches itself from the body, complete with digestive tract, and flies —'

Webb shook his head. 'Sorry, I'm . . . I'm not fully with you. Are you saying that — ?'

'I'm just telling you what North believed,' White interrupted. 'Whilst at the same time trying to get to the bottom of this case. This was no ordinary murder, of that I'm certain. Amongst North's possessions was a bag filled with broken bottles. Glass shards. Now in the book it states that one way to kill one of these things is by stuffing the headless corpse with glass, thus preventing the — '

'Will you just listen to yourself for a moment, Detective? Hell, I thought you guys were supposed to be, well, if you don't mind me saying it, rational. You're making this sound like something from a bloody horror film.'

Tiredly, White rubbed his head. 'Yeah, I guess you're right. Maybe I've been working too damn hard. Everybody's been putting in the hours trying to apprehend this dreadful child-snatcher.'

'The best thing you can do is go home and rest. No doubt in the morning you'll feel better, and you can go over this with Doctor Laidler.' Webb sniffed the air. That acetic acid reek was getting stronger.

'I guess you're right.' White stood up. 'Well, I'll be going, but if you need to get me here's my number.' He handed over a small white card. 'If you can leave a message for Doctor Laidler informing him that I'll drop by around ten, I'd appreciate it.' He turned and left, obviously eager to be going.

★　★　★

It was only after the detective had gone that Webb noticed he had forgotten to take the book. He picked it up and began reading. He had only got to the third page when the door to the morgue crashed open and White rushed in, his gun in his hand.

Webb opened the office door. 'Detective?'

'She's here! That bitch is here!'

'What?'

'Your receptionist's dead and so are two nurses. Boon-Mee's come back for her body!' White was on the edge of hysteria, his eyes darting in every direction.

Fear bubbled in Webb's mind as he stared at the detective, his mind spinning madly.

'We've got to get out of here!'

'What?'

'Do you want to die?' asked White pointedly.

With wooden steps, Webb stumbled forward. What the hell was going on? There was a sudden tightness in his throat and he swayed for a moment, unable to come to terms with everything that was unfolding. 'No, of course not, but — ?'

'Then let's go. Let's get out of this place.'

'Okay, okay.' The last thing Webb wanted to do was get on the wrong side of a man whom he now believed was mentally unhinged. More so as the man in question had a gun.

'Come on, then.'

A riot of chaotic thoughts was swirling around in Webb's brain as he left the morgue and stepped out into the corridor.

'I've already called for backup,' said White.

'That's — ' Webb stopped. Up ahead, lying face down in a puddle of blood, was one of the late-night nurses — an attractive young woman called Stacey Hopkins with whom he had shared many an intimate moment. He broke into a staggering run and knelt down at her ravaged corpse. 'What the hell?' There was no pulse. She was as dead as dead could be.

White screamed. Webb looked up from the mangled corpse.

From around the corner, where the stairs led up to the ground floor, floated a truly nightmarish vision — the penanggalan. Its gruesome appearance was more or less as North had depicted it in his book. The head was that of a dusky red-eyed Oriental woman, her facial features twisted and bestial, her black hair long and parted down the middle. Like a jellyfish's tentacles, from the stump of her neck trailed a grisly growth of unsightly

189

entrails and organs. The thing hissed, exposing its sharp fangs as it saw the two men.

Webb cursed volubly as he scrambled back to his feet. Now that he had seen that unearthly, utterly horrendous thing in the flesh, it would be unlikely that he would ever sleep comfortably again.

White raised his gun and shot off three bullets. With an unholy screech, the penanggalan sped forward. Screaming, both men turned and fled.

Webb was the faster. He flung the morgue door open and leapt inside. The detective was close behind. He had only just crossed the threshold when the disembodied head reared high above him and launched down, its maw agape. A second later, White roared in agony as the fanged mouth clamped down on his throat.

Webb stared helplessly as the penanggalan sank its sharp teeth deeper, latching itself firmly on to its victim. To his horror, he saw the thing's dangling innards take on a life of their own, coiling around the unfortunate detective, entwining him like some terrible vine, drenching him in blood.

Despite the fact that its now heavily bloodied mouth was otherwise occupied, sucking
the life from its prey, an evil sounding
laugh was coming from it.

Struggling violently, the detective was
dragged away from the morgue entrance.
His feet skidded in a pool of blood and he
went down. Still the fiend bit into him.
Blood sprayed from his severed carotid
artery. Ferociously, he was shaken like a
rag doll in the jaws of a vicious
Rottweiler.

Webb dashed forward and slammed the
morgue door shut. He snatched up a
nearby chair and wedged it. Frantically,
he searched for anything that might prove
of use — anything he could employ as a
weapon. His eyes fell on a bone saw.

The door juddered but held firm.
Blood seeped from beneath it, trickling
along the tiled floor.

Snatching up the saw, Webb pulled
back further from the door. A dark wave
of adrenaline surged through him as he
mentally wrestled with all that he had
seen. Breathing heavily, he stood transfixed, staring at the closed door, a cold

sweat bubbling to the surface of his skin. This was not happening, he tried to tell himself. His mind suddenly lurched and for a moment his vision swam, then darkened. He felt incredibly dizzy as a bout of nausea threatened to overcome him. Reaching out for a nearby wall, he managed to support himself.

All was quiet.

Nerves afire, Webb somehow staggered back to his office. Mind reeling, he sank into his chair. He felt unnaturally cold, but there was a filming of sweat on his face. A peal of hideous laughter gurgled in the depths of his mind. There was the sensation of evil around him, crowding in from every direction.

There came a sudden clatter from the operating theatre. Webb sprang to his feet and rushed to the office door. With grasping ugly claws, horror tore through his brain as he saw the headless disembowelled cadaver of Boon-Mee, having fallen from the operating table, get clumsily to its feet. A sudden madness took hold. Yelling insanely, he rushed out and, gripping the bone saw, hacked down at the decapitated zombie, the serrated edge of the heavy surgical instrument embedding deep into the thing's left shoulder.

The decapitated corpse stumbled, pale arms which should have succumbed to rigor mortis reaching out, trying to grab the one attacking it. A clawed hand flashed before Webb's face. He withdrew the bone saw and savagely hacked down a second time, enlarging the wound at the shoulder. With a cry of rage, he pulled, slicing through flesh and bone. The stench of vinegar was almost overpowering.

Something thumped heavily against the door, the loud bashing accompanied by a wailing scream. Boon-Mee's headless body fell to the floor. It was trying desperately to get to the door, to let its other body part in.

Webb sat astride the fiercely bucking corpse. A blood-crazed madness had now taken possession of him, for he was now hacking with abandon. Blood streamed from his face and there was a mad look in his eyes as, like a butcher with a carcass, he repeatedly chopped down. He then began sawing at the arm.

Soul-wrenching screams accompanied a frenzied battering at the morgue door. Frantically cutting through the bone, Webb severed the cadaver's left arm. The chair which he had blocked the entrance with went flying. His heart almost stopped beating as he looked up, his gaze rising from the trailing intestines and leaking innards to the monstrous head which perched at the top. Madly, he sprang forward and slammed the door on the advancing horror. Unaware of the sounds of his own screams, he applied his strength to keeping the penanggalan out.

The one-armed, acephalous body began crawling forwards, its actions weakening. Webb could see that around the neck stump a milky white liquid was frothing and dripping. It was this secretion which exuded the pungent, almost lachrymatory stink of vinegar. Even in his maddened state, he was drawn to the conclusion that this lubricatory fluid was being released in readiness for the re-attachment process of head and body.

Still the horror banged at the door,

butting it, needing to get in.

There came a scream from outside — a man's scream.

The pressure on the door ceased, and Webb could only assume that another doctor had arrived on the scene and that the penanggalan had gone in pursuit. Poor bastard, he thought. Still, it gave him a few moments. Knowing that to venture outside would be fatal, he looked for somewhere to hide. He could just lie on one of the spare operating tables, pull a sheet over himself and hope, or —

His eyes were drawn to the morgue lockers. Hurriedly, he ran over to the twenty or so metal cabinet doors and, like a contestant in some warped game show, began opening them. But these did not contain prizes; just the cold white-grey faces of dead men, women and children. All of those on the bottom row were filled. Heart thumping, he finally found an empty locker. Next came the awkward procedure of getting inside. Feet first, on his back, he pushed against the walls of the locker.

The storage compartment slid forward.

It caught on something, refusing to go any further. Web was now half-in, half-out. He cursed, suddenly remembering that several of these lockers did not close properly. Frantically, he pushed. Still the metal tray on which he lay would not budge. Then it gave a little, sliding forward on its rollers. It was now just his head and shoulders that stuck out. If his situation was not as deadly serious, things could have been farcical.

The door to the morgue burst open.

A moment later, Webb gave a final heave and the locker slipped mercifully into place, plunging him into darkness. He felt like a lump of meat going into an oven. He lay there, hoping against hope that he had been quick enough. If not . . .

A terrible caterwaul-like screech shattered the silence. Webb dared not breathe. There came another scream, and he had a mental image of the penanggalan staring down at its one-armed autopsy-scarred body. There came a series of loud crashes, and he knew that in its rage the foul being was wrecking the place in its search for him.

After a minute, or so there fell a disturbing silence. It was during this time that Webb feared the most for his life and sanity. This was assuredly worse, far worse than being buried alive; knowing that at any moment the locker in which he hid could be slowly drawn back and that he would find himself staring up at that unbelievably hideous abomination. In such a position he would be vulnerable, unable to move, trapped, completely at its mercy.

He could envisage the loathsome creature floating around the morgue like some grotesque fairground balloon, its horrible hanging looped viscera the string.

The sound which followed was truly disgusting. A wet squelching noise. There was a final pop and then the faint sound of bare feet running.

Five, then ten minutes passed.

Straining every sense, Webb lay motionless. All was quiet. Dimly, very dimly, he thought he could hear the sound of police sirens. He waited a while longer. Then, when he reasoned the coast was clear, he gave a gentle push.

The locker door was jammed.

Webb cursed. He pushed harder. The tray on which he lay did not budge. A ripple of insane laughter came to his lips as he realised he was now well and truly stuck.

*   *   *

His lab coat blood-spattered, Webb was still laughing to himself when the locker was eventually forced open by two obviously apprehensive cops. He was rolled out and helped upright.

'All right, buddy. Would you care to tell us what happened here?'

'You wouldn't believe me if I told you,' Webb answered, only vaguely aware that there was at least one gun levelled at him. He could see that Boon-Mee's mutilated cadaver was no longer on the floor and, as he was led away, gibbering and giggling, he noticed that Detective White's coat was also missing.

THE LAST NIGHT
OF OCTOBER

When the streets ran red with blood . . .

The sun was fast disappearing behind the hills and a cold wind sent the dry leaves hurrying over the road as Edward Haigh changed gears and allowed his battered car to proceed down the steep slope almost under its own momentum. According to his map, nestled somewhere in the gathering gloom below him lay the village of Kirkwick, an isolated settlement of less than a hundred inhabitants. This part of Northern England, somewhere close to the Cumbrian-Northumberland border, consisted for the main of huge tracts of desolate undulating countryside, shadow-filled glens, deeply forested valleys and mile after mile of drystone wall, with a few scattered farms lying tucked away behind the tall hedgerows.

Tonight it was All Hallows Eve. Even the name had a distinctly frightening ring about it. He turned it over and over in his mind as he drove along the narrow winding road through the darkening countryside. This was the night when, in the old days, every door had been shut against the evil spirits; when jack-o'-lanterns and garlic had been placed on lintels to keep away the dead and the creatures of the night; when it was believed demons rode the night wind, seeking souls.

As an expert on rural folklore, Haigh knew that witchcraft and fouler occult practices had once been rife in these parts. He had done his research, discovering that it was here in this very village that the last witch in England had supposedly been burned at the stake. There was a stone in the village square which commemorated this. The sole public house in Kirkwick was even named The Burning Witch.

Haigh gazed through the black lengthening shadows which lay across the road. He seemed to have driven further than he had estimated from the map. Then, as he mounted a low rise and started down the other side, he saw in the distance the church spire rising high above the roofs of the houses clustered around it, as though they were seeking the protection of its proximity. Squinting, he noticed that the tip of the spire was still blazoned with scarlet as the last rays of the setting sun touched it with blood-red fingers.

Five minutes later, he drove into Kirkwick, passed The Burning Witch and stopped the wheezing engine of the car. It shuddered for a moment, then died completely. There were few people in the street and those that he saw seemed to be hurrying to get back home.

Getting out of the car, he slammed the door shut and looked about him. Why was everyone in such a rush? One could almost think they were afraid.

Shifting his gaze from the scurrying pedestrians, he scanned the street, noticing the sign of a small rundown hotel.

He paused for only a moment, then pushed wide the door and strode purposefully into the lobby. There was no one inside, but just as he reached the desk, a door at the back opened and a fat ugly man shuffled forward behind the counter, eyeing him curiously. Behind him, peering nervously, was an elderly woman, presumably the man's wife. Her skin was grey, the colour of her bedraggled hair.

'Stoddard's the name. What do you want?' said the hotel owner through a largely toothless mouth, emitting a foul waft of halitosis.

'I'd like a room,' said Haigh brusquely.

'None available.' With two fingers, Stoddard burst a lump below his bottom lip.

'Is that so?' Haigh reached forward before the other could stop him and pulled the register towards him, turning it quickly and scanning down the page. 'Just as I thought. You don't have any guests here at all. I hardly expected any at this time of year, in this out-of-the-way place.' He stared fixedly yet disdainfully at the man.

'Well, I . . . I guess I was mistaken. We do have two rooms available now that you draw my attention to it. However, you realise that we find it extremely difficult to engage decent staff here in such a small village and, well, consequently, service is both bad and slow. Take my word for it, this isn't the kind of place you'd want to stay at. There's nothing for the likes of you here.' Stoddard shook his head, his bulldog-like jowls juddering. He dabbed at the bleeding sore on his chin and examined the discharge on his fingers. 'Of course, if you've a car, I'd recommend you drive on to Penrith or Carlisle. There you'll find excellent hotels.'

Haigh eyed the unfriendly pair coldly, his eyes narrowing. 'If it wasn't for the fact that it would be so ridiculous, I'd say that you're deliberately turning away custom.' He planted his palms on the desk. 'Do you always make a habit of this?' He smiled, the action no more than a curl of his lips.

'I'm afraid I don't quite understand.' There was something at the back of the man's eyes which might almost have been fear, and his manner and voice showed signs of agitation. Haigh noticed the way in which his gaze continually flicked to the clock on the wall at the rear of the room, almost as if it were slowly ticking away the seconds and minutes of his life, and he was acutely aware of it.

'Now,' said Haigh tightly, beginning to lose his patience, 'I've driven along some of the worst roads I've ever known, and this, as far as I know, is the only accommodation in Kirkwick, so I'm afraid there's nowhere else I can go. You've spare rooms, you admitted that yourself, and I'm willing to pay any reasonable sum for somewhere to spend the night.'

'It isn't that. Any other time we would be delighted to have you here. We get so few strangers in these parts. But, tonight — well, things are a little different. You understand?'

'I'm afraid that I understand nothing of the kind,' remarked Haigh angrily. He went on: 'Either you tell me exactly why I shouldn't stay here tonight, or give me a room.'

Stoddard sighed and shrugged his weighty shoulders resignedly. 'Very well, if that's what you wish. But don't say I didn't warn you. We don't do food, so if you're after something to eat you'll have to go to The Burning Witch just along the road. They stop serving at eight, so you've plenty of time.'

Haigh signed the register with a flourish, then took the key which the other reluctantly handed to him. 'Your room is the first on the left along the corridor at the top of the stairs.'

The room, Haigh discovered, was as small as he had expected, but well furnished, and the bed was soft and looked comfortable. Not that he intended to sleep.

After depositing his overnight bag, he left the hotel. Twilight was now giving way to full-blown darkness. He strode the short distance to the public house, pausing for a moment to examine the curious sign which depicted an unfortunate woman tied to a stake, flames licking at her lower half. Even though the street lighting was poor, he could see that the manner in which it had been done was quite impressive. There was a certain dynamic quality to it which fascinated him. The best part of a minute elapsed before he tore his eyes from it and went to the door.

His entrance went largely unnoticed by the dozen or so locals. If there should be anything here which might prove interesting to him, perhaps he could get one of these villagers to talk. They might be reticent about talking to a stranger, of course, but he had met their kind before on many occasions, and he knew that he would be able to handle them.

The meal which the landlord provided a quarter of an hour later proved to be little more than adequate. It was while he was eating that one of the locals got up from his seat in the corner of the room and came over, standing beside the table, looking down at him curiously, a glass of whisky in his hand. He was a chubby bald-headed individual who, from the visible dog collar, was clearly the village priest. From the way he swayed, it was obvious that he had been drinking for some time.

'You're a stranger here,' he slurred.

Haigh nodded. 'Your observation is

correct. Although I've been to Kirkwick before.'

'Then you should've known better than to come here a second time.' Unsteadily, the priest sat down.

'I've come here looking for something, and I don't intend to allow you or anyone else in this village to put me off.'

The other drank deeply from his whisky, then set the glass down and stared at it for a long moment. 'You've come here to find out something about the witch, I suppose.' He seemed to have sobered up slightly.

Haigh smiled a little and felt a slight tremor of excitement pass through him. He hadn't expected the other to talk so frankly. Perhaps he might find something here in this little out-of-the-way village after all — something to make up for all of the disappointments he had experienced in the past.

'You're a witch-hunter, yes?' queried the priest after a brief pause.

Haigh looked him dead in the eyes. 'Does that surprise you?'

'Why, no. I suppose you know what

you're looking for?'

'Perhaps,' Haigh admitted cautiously. 'Naturally I'd heard about her when I came through here some years back. I know that there's a stone in the square commemorating where she was burned at the stake.'

'That's right. Whenever we get anyone here they always ask about her, and almost invariably they go away satisfied and suitably horrified by the story.' The priest paused, took up his drink again and peered at Haigh over the brim of his glass. 'Well I'm sorry to disappoint you but there's nothing that should concern you behind the story. Most of it's just fabricated nonsense — a gruesome little tale passed from father to son, which, over the years, has become . . . mythologised.'

Haigh drained his glass and pushed his empty plate away into the middle of the table. 'So there never was any truth in the tale after all? Is that what you're saying?' Deep down inside, he felt the sinking sensation of defeat which he had known many times before. So it had been nothing more than idle gossip which had been spun by these villagers into a semi-legend, obviously for their own avaricious purposes when they had realised that something like this, some half-forgotten mystery, could help to put their otherwise insignificant village on the map and bring in interested tourists during the summer months.

'Oh, there was an old hag burned here several hundred years ago, there's no doubt about that. But she was no witch, believe me. In those days, as you probably know, any old woman who lived alone came to be regarded as a witch sooner or later. She only needed to make one enemy in the village and she would be denounced, and witnesses would swear to the most vile things to get her tried. That's what happened then. She insulted the village baker who brought an accusation of witchcraft against her. According to the reports of that time, which I have read, she made no effort to defend herself against the charges made. Perhaps she'd been drugged before the trial had begun — that sometimes happened — and after she was found guilty of being in league with the devil, she was burned in the square.'

'But you're quite sure that she was no witch?' Haigh put the question directly to the other.

'Quite certain. She was nothing more than a poor old woman accused of witchcraft on the flimsiest of evidence.'

'I see. So it seems I've come all this way for nothing.'

'Well, maybe not for nothing, you see — '

At that moment, the landlord came over with a second bottle of wine and placed it beside Haigh. 'I trust Father Wilfred isn't annoying you,' he said quickly. There was a strange look on his face. 'But sometimes he talks too much. His mind is befuddled, and the more he drinks, the more he imagines he tells the truth.'

'He was telling me that the witch who was burned here was merely an innocent old woman.'

For an instant, a look of relief flashed over the landlord's features as he nodded swiftly. 'That much is true. All this talk of witches and witchcraft is bad for us all. They used to say that it would bring in tourists, people with money to spend, and that Kirkwick would become rich in a very short time. A bit like that 'Last Drop' attraction they've got down Pendle way. But it never did, and the sooner we all forget about these things, the better for everyone concerned.'

'Ah, but you're forgetting about Amelia,' exclaimed the priest, sitting up straight in his chair. 'And if our friend here is to remain in the village tonight, then he must be told.'

'Be quiet, you old fool,' snapped the landlord hurriedly. 'I'm sure he isn't interested in your stupid tales and rumours.' He turned to Haigh. 'I apologise. Our village priest's old and now lives too much in the past and at times, his mind . . . ' He left the remainder of his sentence unsaid, but the implications behind it were perfectly clear.

'Old am I? Simple in the head, is it?' With an effort, the other was on his feet, scraping back his chair. 'Perhaps it's because you're all so afraid of what's going to happen tonight. Yes — ' He looked down swiftly at Haigh, eyes flashing fiercely. 'Tonight is All Hallows Eve. The pagan festival of Samhain.'

'I know that,' began Haigh. 'But I don't understand, you said that — '

'There's nothing whatever to understand,' interrupted the landlord quickly; a trifle too quickly. 'These are nothing more than the ravings of a madman.'

'Nevertheless. I'd like to hear them,' said Haigh slowly.

The landlord threw the clergyman a warning glance, then turned abruptly on his heel and walked back to the bar.

The priest watched him go with a faint sneer on his face. 'Fool!' he said harshly, spitting the word out. 'You must forgive him, but like all the others in the village tonight, he's afraid.'

'Of what?'

'Of Amelia; the horror in the church.' If the other had leaned forward and said the words melodramatically, Haigh might not have believed him; but the casual, simple manner made it more credible. 'Tonight is the one night a year she gets out.'

'Sounds intriguing.' Haigh looked at him closely, then poured himself another glass of wine. 'Would you care to tell me about it?'

There was a momentary hesitation on the priest's part. Then he nodded. 'You'll no doubt find out most of it for yourself very soon. But perhaps if you were to know something about it, before anything happens, it may help you to understand. Amelia Cranswell lived in Croglin, a village not far from here. Legend has it that in 1685 she was attacked by a vampire whilst she lay in her bed. Her screams awakened her brothers, who chased it from the grange, out towards a disused crypt in the nearby graveyard. Allegedly, once they had cornered the fiend, they shot it, drove a stake through its heart, chopped off its head and burned the body.'

'And what became of the woman, Amelia?'

'She . . . '

'She became one of the undead?' Haigh's eyes were suddenly drawn to a nearby window as a figure carrying a flaming torch passed by. From the shadowy movement and the sounds, it appeared that something was going on outside.

The priest noticed the other's curious look. 'That'll be them getting ready for the street party. The villagers have one every All Hallows Eve, even though every year I warn them to stay indoors. But they don't listen. It's as though they forget the annual horror that befalls Kirkwick.'

'You're beginning to interest me,' said Haigh quietly. 'This Amelia — I take it she came here?'

'Yes. Originally it was claimed that she was taken to Switzerland in order to recover from the shock of her ordeal; but her brothers, once they discovered she was cursed with vampirism, were unable to bring themselves to destroy her. She was brought here to the church instead, when they realised nothing could be done to save her. For nigh on three hundred years she's been kept in the vaults below the church. Neither myself, nor any of my predecessors or anyone else for that matter, has been able to destroy her. All of the conventional methods — the stake through the heart, beheading, burning, mouth filled with garlic cloves, dousing in holy water — have proved ineffectual. Which leads me to doubt that the original vampire was destroyed by her brothers.'

'Why do you let her out?'

'What makes you think I let her out? I don't let her out,' Father Wilfred said, shaking his head with indignation. 'Do you think I would willingly let such a creature loose? It's just that on this night, when the forces of darkness are at their strongest, she reawakens and there's nothing that I, or anyone else, can do to prevent it. That's why I come here. In order to get away from the church. I get drunk and stay here till sunrise. It's safer that way. I've been doing this for the past thirty-five years. It's a pity that none of the villagers heed my warning. But as I said, it's as though they've fallen under some kind of a spell — a curse, perhaps; for in the morning, you can be sure that she'll have claimed several victims. Yes, they'll be mourned, but within a week or two everyone will have forgotten what happened.'

★   ★   ★

All of the villagers, except the priest, seemed to be there in the chill darkness; torch-bearing figures, their faces covered by grotesque masks and wearing hideous costumes. A large float moved slowly and ponderously along the narrow, winding, cobbled streets, pulled by a pair of large strong horses. On the float, which had been draped with growths of black ivy, was a witch on a broomstick soaring high against a painted circular moon. The face of the witch was not that of a wizened crone as Haigh had expected, but that of a beautiful young girl. However, her features had been subtly distorted so as to make a horrible and crazy caricature of real beauty. A dozen young children, six on either side, had been done up to resemble medieval plague victims, their grey-green faces covered with leaking boils and filthy bandages. There was an unsettling eeriness to the scene which was compounded by the relative silence which accompanied its passing. None of the children laughed or spoke, almost as though they really were victims dying from some horrible condition. The fact that those on the float numbered thirteen — the unholy number for the witch's coven — did not go unnoticed by Haigh.

Carrying lanterns and flaming torches in their hands, holding them aloft, the villagers crowded around the slowly moving float as it paraded the whole length of the village street. The young and the old followed closely behind the ghoulish procession, their uncanny inhumanly masked faces glowing weirdly in the flickering light.

'Don't you think they're rather like children, playing a strange game that they don't really understand?'

Haigh whirled at the croaky voice, peering into the darkness. He had not heard anyone approach but told himself that the creaking wheels of the float would have drowned out the sound of footsteps. The old hunchbacked man was standing a few feet away in a doorway, peering up at him through rheumy eyes like an aged mole. Like himself, he did not wear a mask.

The old man shrugged his shoulders disdainfully. 'They're all fools! What do they hope to gain by all this? Is it because they're afraid of what will happen and they hope that this display will ward off the evil hour?'

'Perhaps,' Haigh answered. 'And who are you?'

'I'm Victor Crowmarsh, the sexton. You're a stranger here, aren't you? I could be wrong, but I get the impression that you're secretly longing for something to happen. Something other than this pathetic masquerade.'

Haigh nodded. 'For many years I've been examining reports of witchcraft, hauntings, and any other supernatural phenomena; but they have all turned out to be either elaborate hoaxes or there has been a quite natural explanation. I came here several years ago and first heard of the witch then. I thought that perhaps tonight I might see or hear something which I couldn't possibly explain. So far, I've heard only dark rumours and seen this.' He waved his hand in the direction of the procession.

'Perhaps this is all there is,' suggested the sexton with a sly laugh. While they had been speaking, the floats had drawn up, halting in the village square. From a makeshift stall, a pig-masked villager was handing out bottles of local ale and portions of pumpkin pie.

Haigh stared up to where the church brooded over everything, dark and sombre against the night sky. There was a moon low down, and it was just possible to make out some of the details. 'I don't think so,' he said thickly 'After all that I've heard tonight, there has to be something in these old legends.'

Crowmarsh grinned. 'Then if you think that, take a look about you. Study the faces of these people — closely. What do you see?'

For a moment, Haigh stared at the sexton in surprise. There had been a strange intensity in his voice which seemed oddly out of place. Then he turned his head and glanced at a bearded man who stood a few feet away, watching the floats, his head turned away a little. The mask which the other wore looked incredibly lifelike, almost as if it had been painted on. The goat horns sprouting from the forehead, pointed and curved, might almost have grown out of the bony ridge of his skull. The bearded man turned and the goat's lips drew back in a fiendish sneer, revealing twisted brown-stained teeth. A baying neigh came from the open mouth. Now that the drink was flowing, everywhere he looked it was the same. Weird inhuman creatures, dancing and cavorting around the floats, men and women with the heads of beasts.

'I think you'd better come with me.' Crowmarsh tugged at his sleeve. 'Away from all this madness. I'll take you to what you came here to find.'

Haigh found himself unable to answer. His mind reeled slightly, but was oddly clear. The hideously warped beings before his eyes melted back into normal mask-wearing people. It had just been a phantasm; an illusion. A terrible laughter bubbled up from the darkness directly ahead of him, and he realised that the old man had been leading him away from that demoniacal scene of horror in the street, up towards the church which towered broodingly over everything. 'Where are we going?' he asked.

'I thought you wanted to see everything,' Crowmarsh said softly. 'Well, I'm the only one who can show you that.'

Then, with almost startling abruptness, the huge black shadow of the bell in the church tower began to boom the hour. Nine deep shuddering echoes that rattled eerily through the darkness. A mist came and went about the steeple, momentarily erasing its stark shape and the out-jutting stone gargoyles that stared down with sightless eyes.

The wind was soft, whimpering a little bit, a lonely sound between the headstones that reared on either side. Every few minutes, it would mutter and grumble under the shadow branches of a gently bending elm, right up to the vast stone shape of the church itself.

There was a sudden pressure in

Haigh's chest. His arms were tingling. As he climbed the narrow twisting stairway leading up to the top of the church, he glanced back over his shoulder and saw the flickering cluster of lanterns were still there, like a lot of corpse candles clustered around the village square. All was quiet, and there was only the faint sound of their own feet on the path. Presently, they reached the summit. The moon had risen above the horizon now and flooded everything with a weird bilious glow. He paused and looked about him, then turned to face the sexton.

For a moment, the other regarded him in silence, a curiously malevolent look on his face. Haigh slowly shook his head. Something dark and terrible seemed to be lurking out there, very close. The sense of excitement had not faded once they had left the village behind and climbed up into the still blackness; and in a fearsome instant of deeper darkness and understanding, he remembered how the landlord back at the hotel had warned him. His legs were stiff, his arms remained at his side, fingers clawed, nails digging into the flesh of his palms.

Some invisible force seemed to be clamping itself about him, holding him there, trying to root him to the spot.

The white face of the moon was blacked out for several seconds by the racing, scudding clouds. A black shadow-pattern lay across the quietude. The graves were no longer white stone faces that leered at them hungrily through the mist. Instead, they were dark blocks of granite and carved stone and silence; evil, menacing fingers of night that ringed them around. The influence on him eased gradually and he managed to shake it off.

'Around the back of the church is a door to which I have the key.'

'I see. And I take it there's something inside that you think I will find of interest?'

'Oh, without doubt.' Crowmarsh reached into a trouser pocket and removed a large rusty key. 'I'll admit that being up here on a night like this isn't for the faint-hearted, but believe me what you're about to see will make it all worthwhile.'

'And what exactly is that, may I ask?' questioned Haigh tensely.

Crowmarsh turned. 'Ah, you'll see soon enough. I wouldn't want to give the surprise away now, would I?' He had led Haigh to a place where a flight of stone steps descended into darkness. From inside a coat pocket he removed a flashlight and switched it on, shining the beam down to where the stairs ended at an ancient-looking door. He then panned the flashlight over the near wall of the church, illuminating a large stained-glass window. 'If you look carefully enough,' he said, taking Haigh by an arm and steering him so that the other could be in a better position, 'you can see a very strange depiction of our Saviour. There! In that far left corner.'

Hands in pockets, Haigh stared up to where the other pointed.

It was at that moment that the heavy flashlight came crashing down on his head.

★　★　★

Haigh had been neither hurt nor surprised by the violence that had been directed towards him. He had been dragged down the stairs, had heard the door being unlocked, and then he had been pushed inside. It hadn't been the most ceremonial of entrances, but he knew that he would not have been able to enter the church of his own volition.

It was perfectly clear that the sexton had lined him up as a sacrificial offering to Amelia. No doubt it was all a necessary part in reawakening her — so that she could indulge in her once-a-year orgy of destruction. Although it was highly feasible that the festival of Samhain provided her with the unholy strength to permit emancipation, it was also possible that the villagers colluded in this, aware perhaps that this annual bloodfest at least satiated her and kept her from attacking at whim. They would rather feed her once a year than live in constant fear.

It was as black as midnight down here, but to one such as he that posed no problem at all. Looking around him, Haigh could see that he was in a stretch of passage, its walls adorned in places with faded murals. He edged his way deeper into the bowels, the air becoming colder with each step.

Soon he came to the yawning mouth of yet another flight of steps, pausing for a moment in order to look at the malign and deviant images which stared out at him from the crumbling brickwork all around. Slowly and carefully, he began down the steps. Deeper and deeper he went, into the very foundations of the church. Had he still been in possession of his soul, Haigh would no doubt have felt the unholy chill which gusted throughout these nightmarish catacombs. Stepping into a large vaulted chamber, he saw the many stone sarcophagi which lay to either side.

Striding down the central aisle of this dreary mausoleum, Haigh was strongly aware of the hatred which, like a dark flood, seemed to spew out in waves from some of the carved granite and black marble coffins, channelled by the deceased priests who were interred herein. Yet he knew they were impotent, unable to harm him or the one he was about to invoke. That she had not arisen was undoubtedly due to the fact that she hadn't sensed his presence. Had he been a hapless villager, then there was little doubt that he would be dead by now.

In the hushed silence, he knelt before one particularly grimly carved tomb. 'Amelia, my love. I have come to awaken you, to free you from this foul place,' he uttered. 'Even though your brothers staked me, beheaded me and reduced my body to ashes, I vowed I would return to make you mine. It has taken me nigh on three hundred years to reform, during which time I have shared your torment. Together, we will wreak our vengeance on those who have kept you here.'

A dark bluish light began to appear in a beam around the sarcophagus, bathing the stone funerary container in an indigo glare. Shadows slowly coalesced into rigid discernible shapes. Haigh watched as the glow began to shift and transform.

A young woman's spectral face blurred into view. She looked utterly terrified, identical almost to how she had looked three centuries ago when he had first set eyes on her, peering in through her latticed window. Slowly her expression changed to one of intense evil. Her eyes blazed with recognition and a hunger that made even his dead heart leap.

★　★　★

The next morning, Father Wilfred woke slowly with a cold autumnal sunlight pouring in through the wide window, and an opaque pattern of frost-crystals on the pane. He reached out for his coat and shoes and dressed hurriedly. At the back of his mind was a tiny thought, a sensing that something horrible was going to happen — or had happened. It had been a long night, one filled with screams and shouts that had stretched like a dark eternity — a nightmare in which he had imagined all sorts of horrors. He had heard the sounds of frantic hammering as though some had been battering at the door to get in, but he had been both too drunk and too frightened to answer their calls.

Then he remembered. Last night had been All Hallows Eve. That evil indestructible thing — that accursed vampiress

230

from Croglin, the abomination from the church — would have been abroad. The memory still left remnants of fear and madness inside him. He called out, surprised not to find the landlord or any of his helpers. A savage pounding headache beat remorselessly at his temples as he approached the door. Fear bubbled up inside his brain, frothing over, foul with the thoughts that came boiling to the surface. Panic was back, building up thickly in his throat. His hands clenched tightly, his palms suddenly hot and clammy.

A rivulet of blood seeped from beneath the door, congealing in an obscene puddle. Grimacing, the priest stared down. Reluctantly, he reached out for the handle, twisting it in nerveless fingers before pulling the door towards him.

With a suddenness that made him jump, he found himself having to leap clear as a ravaged corpse which had been slumped against the door fell over the threshold. Despite the brutal degree of mutilation, he recognised Henry Jarvis, the school teacher. One of his arms had been torn out at the socket and his bloody face and torso bore deep lacerations; claw-marks. The hideous mask he had worn lay shredded beside him.

He felt sick. The sight, the scale and the savagery of the carnage brought his supper to his throat. Lurching to one side, he vomited, reaching out with a shaking hand to support himself. He felt his legs weaken and quiver beneath him, while his eyes were glued to the grisly remains that lay spread-eagled before him. Fear thickened until it paralysed his thoughts. He could feel his pulse racing. He had to get out — to leave this place of madness. To run, and run, and not stop running. In stumbling movements, he stepped over the body, leaving The Burning Witch.

The village of Kirkwick had become the sight of a massacre, its streets awash with blood.

In the village square, the dead — young and old alike — were strewn all over the place. A scattering of unsightly body parts lay near the overturned float. Even the horses hadn't been spared from this murderous rampage, their disembowelled corpses glistening wetly in the morning sunlight. And sprawled upon the witch's memorial stone were the gory headless remains of the sexton.